Time Hunter

Kelsey Russo

Contents

1. Chapter One — 1

2. Chapter Two — 8

3. Chapter Three — 15

4. Chapter Four — 21

5. Chapter Five — 26

6. Chapter Six — 31

7. Chapter Seven — 35

8. Chapter Eight — 39

9. Chapter Nine — 46

10. Chapter Ten — 52

11. Chapter Eleven — 58

12. Chapter Twelve — 66

13. Chapter Thirteen — 79

14. Chapter Fourteen — 83

15. Chapter Fifteen — 89

16. Chapter Sixteen — 95

17. Chapter Seventeen — 102

18. Chapter Eighteen — 106

19. Chapter Nineteen — 112

20. Chapter Twenty — 117

21. Chapter Twenty-One — 122

22. Chapter Twenty-Two — 127

23. Chapter Twenty-Three — 133

24. Chapter Twenty-Four — 141

25. Chapter Twenty-Five — 147

26. Chapter Twenty-Six — 154

27. Chapter Twenty-Seven — 161

28. Chapter Twenty-Eight — 166

29. Chapter Twenty-Nine — 174

30. Chapter Thirty — 179

31. Chapter Thirty-One — 188

32. Chapter Thirty-Two — 191

33. Chapter Thirty-Three — 197

34. The Next Chapter — 204

35. Timed Out — 205

Chapter One

C hapter One

The world was dying and we only had a little bit longer to find a way to save the planet, or leave. Saving Earth didn't seem like a realistic option. Humans had tried repeatedly and failed. Time was running out. Time. There was that word again.

Tree trunks loomed high overhead as I crept through the ugly remains of what was once a forest. It was quiet. Too quiet. This place, like so many others, had been destroyed by decades of fighting, leaving miles of dirt and empty landscape.

My boots sank into the soft surface with each step, almost causing me to stumble forward as I tried to pull my foot back out. It was hard to imagine this place might have been beautiful at one point. Now, everything was dead.

So much devastation had happened. We, humans, had destroyed our home, and the clock was ticking on when life would cease to exist. It was time to leave this place, but that was easier said than done. Despite technology, we weren't ready to completely abandon our home.

My white suit gleamed in the darkness as I continued to patrol the outer perimeter of OnyxFive. Yes, this ugly place surrounded the facility I currently resided. The others from my team were around; I could feel their energy. We had split up to cover more territory, but I knew they were close, for now. I could imagine their boots also sinking into the dirt as they tried to canvass the area. It had become part of our daily responsibilities.

Stopping behind one of the stumps, I slowly leaned around its burnt edge. I was an easy target in this environment for enemy soldiers, or for the few remaining crazed animals, out in search of a meal. I hated the white suit, but my brother told me repeatedly that it was necessary, and a requirement. Besides, I hadn't seen one normal in the weeks since I had started doing perimeter checks. I almost wondered what it would be like to find one hiding among the dirt hills. Would they attack me? Would I have to fight back?

I sighed. At least, that would be something to do. I was growing increasingly bored with my daily assignments.

A deep voice spoke through my headset. "Esa, where are you?"

I paused, silently debating whether or not to respond. Finally, I realized it was pointless to ignore the voice. He would only ask again.

"I'm in quadrant eight. It's empty," I finally whispered back, continuing to scan the area. Slowly, I crouched a little further behind the stump. A grayish haze drifted through the morning air, making it difficult to see.

"Thank you. I see you now," the smooth voice responded.

"That makes me feel better. I always like knowing my every move is being watched," I said, annoyed that I was once again being tracked. Lately, it seemed like more and more people knew my every move.

A small black bug began to travel up my boot toward my leg. I knew it was probably on a desperate search to find another living being, but I really didn't want to be the thing it was looking for right at this moment. I reached down and flicked it off before it could get any closer.

"Come on back. We need to scan you," the voice said. He obviously wasn't getting the point that I didn't want to talk right now.

A deep sigh escaped my mouth. "Why? I just got started." I made no attempt to hide my annoyance that I was being pulled off duty and forced to go back inside. I didn't like being out here, walking around this emptiness looking for anyone or anything that might still be alive, but I hated being inside even more. I felt stifled inside of the facility.

"Captain Esa James, it's an order. Come on back. Now," Paul bellowed. It was a command I knew ultimately it would be a mistake to ignore.

"Fine," I grumbled, tired of being ordered around by him.

I begrudgingly took a few steps in the direction I had just walked, moving from tree stump to tree stump and pausing every few feet to see if I could hear any sounds. I almost wished there was something, so I could prolong my trip back, but there was nothing. It was empty of any life outside of our team and a few bugs.

I touched the medallion that hung on a chain around my neck. The blue vapors of the Jump Line appeared. Instantly, a cool blast of air greeted me as I landed inside OnyxFive's brightly lit exchange room. My arms swung out from my sides as several small beams of light made their way from my head to my toes, inspecting every inch of my body, looking for any intruders that might have made their way onto my suit.

Beep. Beep.

The lights continued until I was cleared to walk into the research facility located in the southern quadrant.

Within, the narrow, brightly lit hallways spanned for miles as men and women in black lab coats rushed along the corridors. Everyone seemed to be in a hurry. They knew the timetable had been shortened and we needed a viable place to go. It had to be a place that could sustain us for centuries, and that seemed to be the hard part. We couldn't find a suitable location.

At one point, Earth was a vibrant planet with different continents, religions, and ethnicities, but now that had changed. One war ended it all, the Century War. In the end, it was science that prevailed—two scientists in particular, who created opposing research facilities: NorthStar and Onyx-Five.

Technically, I guessed I should be happy to finally have a place where I belonged, but there was something about OnyxFive that caused a continuous queasy feeling in my stomach— a feeling that kept me up for hours at night. I'd hoped it would go away, but nothing seemed to help. This was my home.

My brother, Samuel, thought differently about OnyxFive. So, apparently, did the rest of the team, including Theo. Up until a few weeks ago, our team had consisted of six soldiers, but now we were down to five. Three years ago, I had been a captain of our team, but something happened to me while I was on a mission and I got stuck in the twenty-first century. I've since learned my mother had a part in that disappearance. She apparently sent me to kill the ancestors of the previous team member.

My relationship with Theo had gotten better over the past few weeks, but it was still complicated.

Luther, the "traitor," was, for good reason, no longer on the team. In fact, we hadn't been able to find him. Instead of Luther, we now had Paul.

I wasn't sure how to classify General Paul James. It was difficult for me to think of him as one of the good guys, a part of the team, or as my biological father. It was the last part that was the hardest for me to understand. A few years ago, he had apparently been "dad," but somehow our relationship had changed into a working one. Unfortunately, I don't remember the small details. Some recollections had returned when we paid NorthStar a visit, but the rest of my memories past three years ago remained a blank. For now, I only know Paul from when we'd first "re-met" a few months ago. I'd describe the relationship as complicated.

I pulled at a strand of my long, white hair. It was loose today, with a perfect part straight down the middle. Just the way I liked it. Lines are important.

My tall frame and pale skin made me stand out among the "normals" at OnyxFive. There was no doubt something was different about me and the other four on the team...as well as Paul. We were different. Our bodies radiated electricity that elicited fear among some of the scientists when they approached us. Secretly, I enjoyed being able to cause them to quiver.

Samuel's lab was located on the main research floor, near the back of the facility, and since we had arrived, he rarely left the area.

"Where is the rest of the team?" I asked my brother as I strolled into the room, looking to see if any of the others had also been called back inside, but it was only me and Samuel in the room.

Samuel was sitting in his chair, looking at the soft glow of his computer screen. His white hair was longer than usual. A thin strand covered part of his face as he continued to peer back and forth between his computer and a device in his hand. He slowly moved his delicate, pale fingers around the metal object as if he was checking out its smooth cover to detect any flaws.

"They're still out," Samuel responded dryly, though his focus stayed on the object.

I let his statement linger in the air for a few seconds, hoping the uncomfortable silence between us would force him to say more, but he proved me wrong. Again. Samuel had no desire to continue the conversation.

"Why did Paul call me back in?"

Silence.

I knew I shouldn't be surprised; this was the same response he'd given me for the past few weeks. Someone was always just "out." No one ever seemed to want to tell me exactly where they were or why I wasn't included.

Letting out an exasperated sigh, I slowly made my way to the tiny couch in the corner and plopped down on the soft leather. I leaned back, crossed my hands over my chest, and stared at my twin brother. "Any chance you might expand your answer to tell me where everyone else is right now?"

"Esa, I'm busy. Can we talk about this later?"

"Fine." I made sure my brother could hear the annoyance in my voice. "Don't worry, I'll figure it out on my own."

"Okay," he said, finally looking up at me. He seemed tired. His once flawless ivory skin now showed dark blue circles under his eyes.

I grabbed another of his contraptions and rolled the device in my hands. The metal object lit up from the electricity coming from my palms. It was a beautiful sight.

"Esa, stop playing around with that. It's a weapon."

"Whatever." I dropped the contraption, and it instantly returned to its metallic color. "I feel like we should be doing something. We ended up here and we don't seem to really be doing anything other than walking the perimeter and undergoing more scans. What about Luther and Troy? Shouldn't we be out there looking for them?"

Silence again.

Bingo.

Samuel's lack of conversation told me all I needed to know. The team was obviously out there looking for Troy and Luther, but I was stuck here...with my babysitter.

"All right, what's going on? Look at me. Where is the rest of the team?" I demanded, frustrated that, once again, I was being left in the dark.

Samuel glanced over at me and rubbed his temples. "Esa, yes, several members of the team have been looking for Luther."

"So that means everyone but you and me?" My eyes narrowed and locked onto his.

"No. That really means everyone but you," he said, standing and stretching out his arms behind his back.

Two could play this game. Samuel would be sorry he'd crossed me yet again.

Chapter Two

"What? Why?" I questioned, leaping from my seat. My fists clenched tightly, I was ready for a fight. Physical or verbal; it really didn't matter this time.

"Theo didn't think you were strong enough yet. Don't forget, it's only been two months since your return. Luther and Troy are too dangerous and we know they both definitely want you."

"You and Theo are idiots." I seethed as I turned to hide my face from his. Anger ignited my body and I didn't want Samuel to see just how mad I was at this moment. The electricity coursing through my veins was strong right now. Very strong. "I thought I had proved myself when we were at NorthStar."

"Esa, you were strong on that mission, but you also directly disobeyed my orders and changed the plan. It's too risky to have you out in the field."

Before Samuel could say anything else, I pulled out my medallion and opened the Jump Line. Beautiful swirls of various shades of blue vapors danced in the small lab as I ran onto the line that helped us travel through time, to search for the rest of the team.

"Esa, wait!" I heard Samuel yell, but I had no plans to turn back. He could have just provided me with the information instead of playing another stupid game. Frankly, I didn't need him. I could do this on my own.

I looked down at my watch to see the year 1925 flash on the screen. Honestly, I wasn't sure why that was the year in which I'd landed first, but I needed to start somewhere and it was the first date that popped into my head. Nevertheless, it was empty; I couldn't feel energy from anyone on the team.

Over the past few weeks, I had gotten good at jumping in and out of various places in time without disrupting anything. I hit several key years before my primary year of 2105, trying to feel my teammates' energy, but I wasn't picking up anything.

I raised my palm in front of me. A thin line of electricity danced in the middle of it before disappearing back beneath my skin. I was definitely ready if someone tried to attack me while I was on this personal mission.

Finally, I decided to go to the one year that I had tried so desperately to forget: 1910. That was the year in which Luther had killed the team's good friend, Mary, but there was nothing there. It was quiet.

It was in the year 1950 that I finally felt the faint presence of someone else on the line. Quickly, I jumped forward to 1960 and the energy got stronger. I'm getting closer. I'll find you guys.

In 1965, the energy was very strong. My entire body tingled from the new source on the Line. There was no denying that at least two members of the team were somewhere in this year. Gottcha.

The strength of the energy definitely meant it was more than just one of the jumpers, but who and why? I hadn't heard of any missions scheduled for this year. We didn't need any bodies. We had enough in storage right now to get us through the next few weeks, unless there was some sort of major incident.

A sense of pride washed through me. They could deny it all they wanted, but I was getting good at jumping. Unfortunately, my physical body couldn't seem to keep up with the demand; I was already growing tired from so much traveling. I needed to head back to my primary year, but I would be visiting 1965 again...and very soon.

"Did you find anyone?" Samuel asked as I landed back in his lab.

"What's going on in 1965?" I responded with my own question, crossing my arms over my chest. I had no plans of letting him off easy.

"Hmm. Maybe you are a little better at tracking then I've given you credit for."

"You didn't answer my question."

"We think Luther is hiding out somewhere in that time. He's jumping forward and then heading back to 1965. That's all we know. So far, he's been very effective at covering his tracks, but we agree with you, there is something significant about that year."

The glass sliding door to the lab suddenly slid up and Paul entered the room. His pale skin glowed even whiter today, almost as if he were an ivory statue.

There was part of me that still struggled to believe Paul was a good guy. There was something in the way his steely eyes looked at me and Samuel. We were more than just his children—we were his soldiers, and his most valuable experiments. I wondered if the latter was more important to him.

Just as Paul was about to speak, Theo appeared next to him.

Before either could say anything, I marched over to Theo and landed my fist squarely against his chest. The force of the impact made a loud thud. I pulled back my arm, ready to swing again, but Theo was too quick. His muscular hand completely covered my smaller one, and he looked me in the eyes as he began to squeeze. Then he sent a volt of electricity from his hand into mine. The sensation caused me to jump back.

I was more than a little upset. Theo was once again treating me like a fragile porcelain doll that could break at any moment. "You jerk. You've been out tracking Luther and Troy without me," I said through heavy breaths. I wanted him to say something that would give me more of a reason to dislike him.

"You are not ready, Esa," Theo barked, looking directly into my eyes.

"Like hell I'm not! I'm tired of you all leaving me in the dark." I jerked my hand away from his. "You know that I am ready. This is just your sick way of keeping me locked up here."

"Esa, it was my call," Paul chimed in as he stepped between us. "Theo was just following orders."

I looked over at Theo. His eyes had softened. He silently mouthed, "Sorry."

"Esa, you are not ready. You just jumped to several time zones and came back weak. That's not normal. You should be building up more resistance, with the ability to jump longer and farther," Paul said, his eyes meeting mine. "That is one of the reasons I keep forcing you to get checked. We need to understand what is going on inside your body. It seems like you being gone for three years, may have done something to your internal make-up. You simply are not as strong as the rest of the team."

"You're wrong. All of you are wrong. I am good and you've got to stop treating me like a broken child." I spun and abruptly left Samuel's lab.

The hallway was quiet as I stormed toward my room. It was among a cluster of others in the living quarters. Each person had a small room with a bed and a bathroom. Nothing too luxurious, but at least we had privacy; although, I had a feeling each of the rooms was heavily monitored.

I walked down two more hallways without passing anyone. That was odd. Usually there were at least two or three people in the corridors. OnyxFive was big, but sometimes it felt too cramped with so many people living and working inside.

The energy in the hallway suddenly changed. Someone from the team was near. I turned to look back down the narrow space, but there was nothing. I must have been imagining it.

Just then something ran by me, causing my hair to blow upward. At the sensation, I stopped abruptly and look around again. Still nothing. Seconds later, there was a soft tap on my shoulder. I froze. I definitely hadn't imagined that! Then was another tap.

"Hello?" I asked. "Who's here?"

Silence.

Then something grabbed a chunk of my hair and pulled my body backwards. I wasn't in the mood for games and swung my fist into the empty space, hoping to hit something.

Pain suddenly exploded at the base of my neck. Something had forcefully grabbed me and was squeezing. I still couldn't see anything, but I could feel it. The energy inside me was intense now. Someone or something stood behind me.

Before I had time to react, I was lifted off the ground. Then I was flying through the air like a rag doll. My head hit the wall with a loud thud and

I crumpled. I tried to force myself to roll over and get up off the ground before I was attacked again.

Too late.

Whatever it was grabbed my right arm and leg and swung me around, throwing me hard against the opposite wall. My head crashed into the hard surface again. Slowly opening my eyes, I tried to see what was in the hallway with me. I kicked at the empty space in front of me, but came up with nothing. I tried to calm my breathing so I could focus and figure out where my attacker was hiding, but nothing seemed to work. Then my assailant lifted me into the air again.

Mustering what strength I could, I let out a piercing scream.

The thing threw me down the hallway and I landed at an unusual angle on my arm. A stinging sensation rushed through me as a large red spot blossomed on my white jumpsuit.

"Esa!" Theo charged down the hallway and kneeled beside me. "What happened?" He looked panicked.

"I don't know," I managed to mumble as the pain set in. My entire body ached. "Something was in the hallway with me, but I couldn't see any-thing."

Paul and Samuel ran up behind Theo. Both were breathing heavily as they crouched near me.

"We need to scan the building and see if there has been any change in the energy levels over the past few minutes." Paul looked over at Samuel.

Samuel nodded and ran back into his lab.

"Esa, I'm not sure if this is going to hurt, but I need to get you back to Samuel's lab." Theo wrapped his arms around me and gingerly picked me up. My head rested comfortably against his large shoulder, but pain rushed through my broken body as the adrenalin began to fade.

Theo carried me to the lab and laid me down on one of the metal tables, before grabbing a pair of scissors and cutting back my jumpsuit. He glanced at Samuel. "It looks bad."

Samuel approached. "Esa, I'm sorry." Before I could respond, he grabbed my arm and pushed the bone back into place, while sending a bolt of electricity through me. My entire upper body felt like it was on fire.

"Aaaaahhhhh!!!" A guttural yell escaped my mouth secondsbefore I passed out.

Chapter Three

I wasn't sure how long I had been out, but the lab was empty when I finally woke. I laid still on the cold metal table, a thousand thoughts running through my head.

Slowly, I willed myself to sit up. My head felt fuzzy and my body ached. I looked down at my injured arm. It had been healed. The pain was gone. A clean white jumpsuit replaced my torn and bloodied one.

Was I dreaming? Had I really been attacked?

I sat motionless on the table as the seconds turned into minutes, trying to figure out what happened and wondering when the team might return. It hit me, they were probably out on some mission and I was stuck here, alone.

My skin tingled as the energy in the room elevated again, and I looked around, wondering who had returned. As far as I could see, I was still alone, but there was no doubt by the amount of energy I was feeling that someone or something was in the room... with me.

Crap. My heart raced as I tried not to panic.

I looked around the room, trying to find something I could use to protect myself, but there was nothing except a few old, odd-shaped projects on which Samuel had been working over the past few weeks.

Then a familiar face with bright pink hair appeared on the opposite wall. "Good morning, Captain James. Is everything all right? Your levels have elevated over the past few seconds."

"LUX, please call Samuel and Theo. Now!" I said, jumping off the table and grabbing the chair near Samuel's desk. This was the only thing in the lab that I could easily throw that might cause my attacker some pain.

The pink-haired sprite-like robot stared back at me. "Samuel has been notified. Captain James, duck!"

The contraption Samuel had been working on earlier in the day hurled through the air, past my head, and hit the glass wall where LUX's face had just been, smashing the screen.

"LUX!" I yelled into the empty room. No other sounds could be heard except my echoing voice. Hurting me was one thing, trying to destroy my favorite computer took this attack to a whole new level.

Before I could move, the table on which I had been lying was forcefully pushed onto its side. The deafening sound of metal hitting the hard floor.

Theo, Samuel and Paul were suddenly standing on the other side of the lab's door, frantic looks on their faces as they tried to open it. Theo began to pound upon the glass wall. Meanwhile, I dropped to the ground and rolled beneath another, smaller table. I'd hoped there would be some sign as to where my attacker was, but again it was quiet.

Just then, there was a loud boom as one of the chairs impacted the door. It hit the unbreakable glass hard, falling with a thud.

Before I could make a move, Theo appeared, grabbed me, and threw me onto the Jump Line.

"What took you so long?" I asked as we arrived in a new place and time.

"Why didn't you jump out of there?" Theo looked back at me questioningly.

"I don't know. I was too stunned by everything that was happening." The realization was setting in for Esa. She should have been smart enough to jump out of that place and away from her attacker.

"We should be safe here for a bit," he said through deep breaths. "It's taking everything right now for me not to go back and try to kill whatever it was attacking you."

"I know." I looked down at my shaking hands. "I feel the same way."

"Esa, my job is to protect you." Theo's pale blue eyes looked sorrowfully into mine.

"And what is my job?" I couldn't help but ask.

He shook his head and then answered in a soft voice. "To be part of the team."

"Do you really want me to be part of the team?" I asked him, wondering if he would answer truthfully.

"Yes. No. I don't know. Watching you get hurt is just too hard."

"Where are we?" I looked around at the new space in front of us.

"I think we are in 2070. I didn't really have time to think of a landing spot. I'm just glad we ended up somewhere quiet."

"It wants to kill me." I shook my head, thinking back to what had happened in Samuel's lab.

"I know," he said, moving closer. "I'm not sure what's going on, but there is definitely something after you, and I intend to find out what it is and destroy it."

"Where were you guys? Why did you leave me alone?"

"We had been in the room, but then we went outside to talk, so we wouldn't wake you. We were looking at some of the scans that had been done on the building. The energy was elevated, indicating that something has found us, but we're still not sure exactly what, or who, is behind the attacks. We hadn't been gone long before we got LUX's call and returned to see furniture being thrown through the air. Obviously, whatever or whoever it was waited until we left to attack."

Theo reached for my hand and entwined our fingers. We sat in silence for several minutes before he spoke again.

"Esa, I failed to protect you before. That won't happen again. There are things I did and said that I'll never be able to take back. When Samuel found you in 2010, I was angry. I was mad at you, at the situation, at everything." He punched the wall, but I could tell he was holding back. He clearly wanted to strike harder, as if to show me how much pain I had caused while I was gone. "But I've learned that it's not you I need to be mad at. Now, I'm just trying to understand the new you."

"I'm sorry," I responded, the words barely audible. It felt like I had said that word so many times of late.

"No. You can stop saying that." His fingers squeezed mine harder. "I know. I'm still trying to process everything. Watching you get attacked back there has sent a new wave of emotions through me."

"Really? Like what?" I asked, surprised by Theo's sudden vulnerability. This was a side of him that only appeared in rare glimpses. He could be normal and nice one minute and the next he was pushing me away...again.

"I'm not doing my job. I'm supposed to protect you, but I haven't been. Three years ago, I should have been more aware that something was going on with Luther. I should have been there to stop everything from happening. Do you know how that feels?" He looked at me with a defeated expression. "Esa, I feel an even bigger responsibility to protect you now that you are different. That's the hard part for me. You used to be so tough and strong, and you are still both of those things, but now you're softer around the edges. I feel like you need me, but I haven't been able to respond."

"That's an interesting way to say that I'm not the same Esa I was several years ago."

"You're definitely not the same Esa, but I'm starting to like the new version better than the old one."

"Really? Why?"

"I just do. It's been nice having you back. At first, I struggled with how different you acted, and I wondered if there was something wrong with you, but over the past few weeks, I've enjoyed getting to know the new you."

I reached up to brush back a lock of his hair as we stared at one another. I wanted to feel safe with Theo, but too much had happened lately.

Theo shook his head. "I have more to say, Esa, but now is not the right time. Lean your head back and try to get some rest. You need to calm your energy so you don't cause a power outage. We'll talk later and figure out a plan for when we return."

"Okay, but don't leave me, Theo. Promise you will stay by my side if I fall asleep."

"I won't leave you."

Chapter Four

The night air was cool against my skin as I walked down the narrow cobblestone path. I remembered this path. It was near Mary's house. The moonlight cast slivers of pale yellow on the trees, lighting the way in front of me. With each step I took, the trees on either side of the path became illuminated. Different colors were everywhere. It was magical. I felt like Alice in Wonderland. My hand trembled as I reached out to touch the branches. Suddenly, it was pitch black. The lights were gone. The trees were dark. Adrenaline coursed through my veins. My breath quicken. I could feel another presence. The Hunter was back.

"Esa, wake up."

Someone shook me. My eyes snapped open to find Theo sitting on the floor next to the chair. He tilted his head slightly before letting out a soft snort.

"That must have been some dream."

My entire body ached as I sat up and tried to get my bearings. It had all seemed so real. "It was a weird dream. I was walking down the path near Mary's house, but it was different. This time, there were lights all around.

It was beautiful." I took a deep breath. "Before I could figure it out, the Hunter was back. I still couldn't see it, but I could feel its energy."

Theo looked at me with a quizzical expression. "Why do you call it 'the Hunter'?"

"I don't know." I slowly shook my head, unsure how to answer his question. "It's a feeling I get. Something is watching and waiting for me to be alone, like a hunter does when it stalks its prey."

Theo stared into the darkness. "I will find out whoever, or whatever, it is and protect you. I promise. You will be safe, Esa."

We sat together in silence for several minutes. It felt good to be near him. Then Theo's breathing grew more rapid and he pulled away.

"We should get back to our primary year. I need to talk to Samuel."

Before I could utter a response, we were back in the lab. The room looked in perfect order. Samuel had already fixed all of the mangled furniture. It was as if nothing had ever happened... but it had.

"I'm glad to see both of you again," he said glancing in our direction.

"Samuel, any idea what that thing was the other day?"

"It's not a what; it's who."

"Who is it?" I prodded, hoping he would give me a real answer for once.

"I'm not entirely sure, but I have a few guesses," Samuel responded, a serious expression on his face.

"Is it Troy or Luther?" I asked. Something told me it had to be one of them. Both had nothing but time on their hands.

"I don't know, but we ran some energy tests and slowed down some video footage. Whoever it was also attacked several of the normals living here and hid their bodies in a closet before coming after Esa."

"Why can't we see him?" Theo asked crossing to Samuel's desk and leaning closer to the computer screen. "It's so frustrating trying to fight something that's invisible."

"That's what I'm still working on." Samuel turned back to his computer.

At that moment, Audrina and Gave stumbled into the lab. Audrina's long white hair was dripping wet and clung to her wet jumpsuit. Gave didn't look any better.

"What happened?" Samuel pushed back his chair and hurried over to Audrina. When he reached her, she fell into his arms. "Aud, what's going on?"

Her eyes were wide. "I don't know. I don't know what happened to me, Samuel. It's all so weird. I think I may be going crazy." She began to shake uncontrollably. "One minute I was jumping off the line, getting ready to come back to our primary year, and the next something threw me into the water and pushed me toward the bottom."

Fresh tears ran down her already tear-streaked face as she sunk further into Samuel's arms. Through her sobs, she finally said, "It was so horrible. Everything happened so fast. Water filled my mouth and I thought I was going to die. Thankfully, Gave grabbed me and we were able to escape."

Samuel looked over at Gave. "What happened? What is Audrina talking about?"

Gave shook his head. "I don't know. I had just seen Audrina on the line, and then she disappeared. I started getting these images of her in the water and went to find her. It was like nothing I've ever experienced before. I was instantly able to find her. I still can't fully explain it."

Gave sank into a nearby chair. "Something is up. This isn't right. I've never had something like this happen to me, where I could see another team member."

Samuel nodded and pushed his glasses up the arch of his nose. "I'd like to run tests on the entire team. Something is happening and I need to know what's going on inside our bodies."

The main door to Samuel's lab suddenly burst open. Paul stood in the doorway with his dark black jacket pulled tightly shut. He scowled at each of us, one by one. "Stop what you all are doing. Follow me. Now."

Theo glared back and crossed his arms defiantly over his chest. "Why? What's going on Paul? It's not like you to barge into Samuel's lab and demand that we follow you."

"Like Captain Samuel James said, we need to run some tests," Paul sneered.

Theo stood his ground. "What kind of tests?"

"You do not have clearance for me to provide you with information on any of our testing methods." Paul responded back at Theo. "Do you want to obey my orders or do you want my soldiers to help you make your decision?"

"How do you know what we were talking about?" I turned toward the man who was supposed to be a member of this team...and my father. He seemed different. There was a definite change in his demeanor. He was more agitated now. The look on his face reminded me of the first time we met. He had that same cold expression then. Of course, I was well aware that Paul was always watching and listening. I just didn't think he would suddenly make it so obvious.

Paul turned on his heels and strode out of the room without answering. A dozen guards holding large guns walked over to us. In a deep voice, one of the guards barked, "Follow us or we will be forced to use these weapons on you."

Samuel looked at each of us, perplexed, and then finally shook his head. "I guess we have no choice but to follow them."

Chapter Five

All five of us got into single file to follow the armed guards. I wondered what Samuel had up his sleeves. He was walking in front of me with his chest puffed out, almost as if he wanted one of the soldiers to say something to him, something that would warrant a response.

The team towered over Paul's army by a good seven to eight inches. Our white suits stood out as we marched down the hallway flanked by black uniforms. We had become prisoners in our own home; if you could really call it that.

We were supposed to be able to live and work at OnyxFive freely—that's what Paul had promised us—but now it seemed he had broken that promise. Everything had changed. I guess I shouldn't be too surprised.

As we rounded the corner, we came into sight of two normals standing in the middle of the hallway, talking to each other. Both turned to look at our large entourage. As we got closer, they each took a step back, confused looks on their faces. The normals were probably wondering why we were being marched like prisoners of war down a hallway we had all walked freely just hours before. I'm sure they thought we had done something criminal; but we hadn't.

We continued to move quietly toward Paul's main lab on the second level. The only sound in the hallway was that of the soldiers' boots against the hard floor.

This seemed a little too easy. Samuel and Theo could have taken out these soldiers already. All five of us were together, and that made us extremely lethal. Why weren't we doing anything?

I glanced over at Paul. Something had changed in his expression. He had to be pondering the same thing. He knew what Samuel was capable of doing to someone he thought was the enemy. It wasn't like anyone on this team to easily give in during a fight.

As we turned down another hallway, I felt the presence of a new energy source. It was strong and approaching us quickly. There was no doubt in my mind: the Hunter was back. He was somewhere in the hallway with us, but we still couldn't see him.

I looked back at Theo. He nodded, his white eyebrows forming an almost perfect "V" and his lips pinched together in a determined scowl. He put his hand on my arm. I could feel his energy coursing through his veins. He must be able to feel the Hunter's presence as well. Audrina glanced back at me, a confused frown on her face. Then her back stiffened.

"Turn around," one of the soldiers barked at her.

Audrina stopped and stared defiantly back at the soldier. "No."

Before the guard could respond, his weapon was abruptly forced out of his hands. It floated in the air, aimed at his head. All of us stood motionless as we waited to see what the next move would be.

The soldier's eyes widened in terror as realization set in that a loaded weapon was aimed at him. He backed up against the wall and stood quietly, slowly he raised his hands in front of his face. Suddenly, another guard lunged for the gun. As one of his hands got close to the floating weapon, it went off.

Bang. The deafening sound echoed down the hallway.

A deep red ooze soaked through the guard's dark uniform as he fell back against the white wall, leaving behind a streak of blood as his body slowly slid to the floor. Almost instantly, the entire hallway erupted into chaos.

Audrina lunged towards another guard. His flesh turned blue as both of her hands came into contact with his body.

I grabbed onto the guard standing next to me and sent a strong current of electricity through his body, causing him to fall to the ground.

Theo, Samuel and Gave all leapt into action. One-by-one Paul's guards were sent to the ground.

The sound of another bullet being released from the gun caused us to abruptly stop. The loaded weapon was still floating in the air. It moved sharply in various directions before rotating back towards one of Paul's few remaining guards.

The guard let out a snide laugh and then ran towards it. Gunfire erupted. We all dropped to the floor to escape becoming the next target.

Samuel grasped his medallion. "Let's get out of here."

Just as he was about to open the Jump Line, an explosion of blinding light erupted in front of us.

Instinctively, I closed my eyes just as I felt something grab my hand and yank me into the brightness. A silent scream escaped from my lips, but then the light disappeared and I opened my eyes to find myself in one of the most beautiful rooms I had ever seen. Samuel, Gave and Audrina appeared next to me. A bewildered look crossed all our faces.

"Where are we? Where did that light come from?"

"I don't know," Audrina responded, as she turned to survey the place in which we'd landed. It was adorned with beautiful white, plush furniture and surrounded by large glass windows that overlooked some sort of ocean. The white tips of the waves glistened in the pale orange sunlight.

"Where's Theo?" I looked around at the rest of the group. We had all made the jump, but Theo wasn't anywhere to be found.

"I don't know," Gave said. "Everything happened so fast. We were on the floor and then we ended up here. I'm not sure what happened."

"Where exactly is here?" I asked again.

"Not sure," Gave said. "I've never seen this place before. It's beautiful, but it's also giving me a creepy feeling."

"I know where we are," Samuel cut in. "I've been here before."

"What?" Audrina asked, flicking a strand of her long white hair off her shoulder. "When have you been here, Samuel?"

Samuel paused and then turned to me. "Esa, there's something I need to tell you. Please don't freak out."

"Why would I freak out?" Samuel was acting weird

"Because I know you," he said, staring intently at me. "I know you will be upset. You always get upset when you think I'm not telling you something."

"What is it, Samuel?" Audrina put her hands on her hips. "Just tell us and stop dragging it out. We don't have time for your long-winded answers right now."

"I didn't tell any of you, but I went and found my mom's research. It included the codes for the Jump Line. There was also something else."

"What?" we all asked in unison.

"I talked to my mother again," he said. "I mean, I talked to our mother, Dr. James."

My hand instinctively flew to the back of my neck where my mom had forever imprinted the code to find her research on time travel. I had known it was only a matter of time before Samuel went and found the items, but I'd assumed he would have told me, so that we could go together. After all, I was the one who was the key, not him. It felt like he had betrayed me by going without my knowledge.

Chapter Six

Had I heard him right? Our mother had visited him again.

"What do you mean?" All of the blood drained from my face and I knew my skin probably looked even more ghostly white.

"I talked to her again," he shrugged his shoulders.

"Where did you talk to her?"

"I was asleep. Suddenly, there was a light above me, like the one we just saw in the hallway. It caused me to blink several times. It scared me at first, but then there was something about the light that was very calming. After what seemed like an eternity a figure appeared. She had long white hair that cascaded down her back. Her eyes were piercing blue, even more blue then mine. I felt like I could see the entire world in them. Esa, there was no doubt it was Mom. Our mom." His voice began to quiver. "She looked amazing."

"Do you think you saw her ghost, or is she alive?" Everything inside of me hoped Samuel would say she was alive, but for some reason, I knew there was more to this story. There was something in his voice. I couldn't put my finger on it right now, but something wasn't adding up.

"No. I don't think she was a ghost. I definitely think she is alive. In fact, the more I think about it, I know she's alive."

"What did she say this time?"

He let out a soft laugh. "Esa, look at me," Samuel said, his voice even more serious. "You need to remember one thing." The creases at the edge of his mouth pulled his lips into an odd-looking smile.

"What?" I asked, glancing around at the rest of the group. All of them were still staring blankly ahead. "What do I need to remember, Samuel? Tell me."

"Things are not always as they seem."

His body began to twitch. His perfect, ivory skin suddenly showed signs of imperfection, almost as if he were a distorted picture on a computer screen. Small blocks of his skin slowly disappeared and he seemed almost pixelated.

I spun toward Audrina, seeking reassurance. She stood stoically in the middle of the room. She, too, didn't look my way. Her body began to twitch.

"No!" I yelled, running over to Audrina, shaking her lean frame, causing her head to flop back and forth with the forceful movement. Finally, her body began to disappear in my hands.

I ran to Gave. Surely he was normal. I looked into his eyes, but they seemed cold...dead. "Gave." I frantically grabbed his face with both my hands. "Please look at me. Please tell me everything is going to be okay," I pleaded.

What was happening? Where were they going?

Gave blankly stared forward. I'd hoped he would give me some sort of answer, but he stood there quietly.

I looked around the rest of the room. Everything began to spin, and my legs grew numb from all the movement. I reached out and tried to grab ahold of something to stabilize me, but it seemed like everything I reached for was inches from my grasp. It was pointless.

"Theo, where are you?" I silently whispered as I tried to slow my breathing and regain my composure. Something was happening. There was no way I was in 2105 right now, but we hadn't made a jump into a different time. We had simply been pulled into the bright light.

As I peered around the swirling room, the windows suddenly changed. Gone was the scene of the beautiful ocean lapping against the glass. Instead, the windows looked out upon thick layers of ice.

Ice was everywhere.

I ran over to Samuel and put my hand on what was left of his shoulder. Normally, a bolt of electricity would release, but this time there was nothing.

Samuel looked into my eyes. "Nice try, Esa, but you aren't strong enough to do anything to me. You are weak."

"I'm not weak!" I yelled as I shoved him. I wanted him to feel some sort of pain, to acknowledge that this was all a dream and that we would soon wake.

He didn't flinch. He just stared back at me. "You are weak, Esa. Weak," he said as his body disappeared completely.

"You are weak, little Miss Esa. Ha ha. You're the weak link. We tried to make you tougher, but it was pointless. You'll never be like the old Esa. She's gone, and now we have you," I heard Audrina's voice mock.

Her body also faded into thin air.

Gave approached and put his hand awkwardly on my shoulder. "Be strong."

"I'm trying, Gave. Help me."

"I can't help you this time. I've tried repeatedly. Now it's time for you to take control."

"No, no, no. I can't do that." I shook my head violently, like a five-year-old in the middle of a temper tantrum. The air in the room had suddenly turned cold. My body trembled from the drop in the heat.

"Gave, help me," I pleaded again. Everything was so confusing right now. I wanted someone to provide me with information.

"I've tried, but it's no use."

"Please, please, please...help me."

"I'm sorry. I can't this time," he said as he slowly disappeared before my eyes.

Gave was gone. Everyone was gone. I was alone again. I wished Theo were here with me. He would tell me what to do. But he wasn't. The entire team had abandoned me.

Chapter Seven

C hapter Seven

The empty room felt massive, like I was a tiny spec of sand in the middle of a vast beach.

My gaze flew to the right and then the left as I tried to get my bearings. There was no doubt someone was watching me. I could feel eyes following my every move. They were close. Someone wanted to see how I would react. I stood stoically in the middle of the room, refusing to give in and let them see any sign of weakness. My eyes snapped shut as I tried to collect my thoughts and calm my beating heart. I reached toward my medallion. I could jump out of this place, but that wouldn't provide me with the answers I needed. Instead, I had to assess the situation so I could figure out my next move.

An eerie quiet surrounded me. Despite my efforts to calm myself down, the opposite happened. My breathing quickened as I thought about what had happened to me and the rest of the team. Everyone was gone. Had they always been a figment of my imagination?

As a second deep breath escaped my lips, I heard an odd commotion coming from somewhere to my right. It sounded as if something was coming towards me at a rapid pace.

My gaze snapped open to see a large, white tiger. Every muscle in its body contracted with each move forward that it made. It slowed its pace when it came within feet of my body.

Its light blue eyes looked deeply into mine as it continued its slow and methodical advance. One step after the other. My feet felt as if they had been glued to the floor. I couldn't move. I wasn't sure if it was the sheer terror I was currently feeling or that my body had lost its ability to ambulate. I was stuck.

I frantically looked around the room, trying to figure out some sort of escape. My fingers again tightened around my medallion. I needed to get out of here. If I didn't, this tiger would have me for dinner. I knew its large teeth were capable of ripping through my soft flesh.

Down near my right leg, I saw the gleam of metal, and I tried to focus in that direction. There was definitely something over there, under the chair. It looked like a large knife.

From somewhere, I heard a deep, smooth voice challenge me. "What do you see?"

I swallowed as I looked back at the tiger.

The voice returned. "Be calm. I don't mean you any harm."

"Who are you?" I asked. "What do you want?"

"It's time for you to learn the truth," the deep voice said again. I could feel the tiger's warm breath on my neck.

"The truth?" I asked, putting my hands on my hips in an attempt to stop them from shaking and give me the appearance of confidence. "Yes, please tell me the truth. It's the one thing I've wanted for a while now."

"I will tell you, but first you need to tell me one thing."

"What?" I asked. I was trying to stay calm, but it was getting increasingly harder.

"You need to tell me your name," the voice said.

"What does that mean?" I responded, annoyed that my name was once again being brought into a conversation, and even more perturbed that I was talking to a tiger whose mouth wasn't moving when it spoke. Was I going crazy? Finally, I managed to utter, "My name is Esa James."

"Wrong!" the voice shot back. "You are wrong. Very, very, very wrong. I thought I had trained you better!"

"No, that's right," I said defiantly. "My name is Esa James."

"No. As I just said, you are wrong. That is not your full name."

"Then why don't you tell me? What is my name?" I asked, scanning the upper portions of the room, wondering where the owner of the voice was sitting, watching me.

"Your name is Captain Esa James. It's the 'captain' part you keep forgetting. It's the 'captain' part that is the reason you disappeared for three years."

I shook from the different emotions I was feeling: hatred, fear, confusion, and irritation. How did this voice know anything about me?

"I haven't forgotten my name." I threw up my fist. The move didn't cause the white beast to flinch. It stood still in front of me, daring me with its eyes to make another move as it gave a low growl.

"Then why didn't you tell me you were one of the captains of the team?"

"I didn't think it was important."

"It's always relevant." I could hear the sneer in its tone. You were created to be strong and lead an elite team of soldiers, but you have failed."

I stared into the tiger's eyes, trying to decide how I should respond. Its eyes were now like a black abyss—inviting, yet hard to look away. It took everything in me to tear my gaze from the darkness.

"I know." I hung my head. I didn't want to hear any more. I was tired of being reminded about why and how I was created. Things had changed since then. "Please stop."

The tiger let out a loud growl that echoed around the room. It was the reaction I was hoping for. In a flash, I saw the gleam of metal under the chair. I threw out my hand to grab ahold of whatever it was, and as I grasped the cool object, a bolt of energy released from my hand.

I threw the electrified object toward the white cat. It didn't move. The metal passed through the beast, causing the tiger's perfect exterior to break into millions of tiny speckles of glitter that slowly fluttered to the ground.

It was gone. I was once again alone.

Chapter Eight

I remained kneeling for several seconds, mentally preparing my next move, in case something else entered the room. I knew I needed to be ready for anything, including jumping out of this place.

The same deep, smooth voice filled the room again. It was hard to tell if the voice was male or female. I guessed that a machine was altering the tone.

"Very good, Captain James. Very good."

"What do you want from me?" I asked, irritated with the games.

"I want you to be strong."

"I am strong!" I yelled. Hadn't the voice seen what I could do? I was lethal and could kill if need be.

"No. You are unsure of yourself. You have moments of clarity, but the rest of the time you are second guessing your capabilities. Watch."

"Watch what?"

"You need to learn how to be patient," the voice said calmly.

A holographic image of a teenage girl appeared in front of me. She had long, dark brown hair and olive skin. Her straight hair was pulled back into a ponytail with a perfect line straight down the middle. Black smudges of dirt covered her face and torn uniform as she ran through a dark, desolate field. The sound of gunfire echoed throughout the area.

She pulled out a gun that had been strapped to her back and fired the weapon at something. I couldn't tell at what she was shooting, but I could see the determination in her eyes. She was aiming to kill. She fell flat on the ground and rolled, while continuing to fire, but this time she turned the weapon in my direction.

A large machine the size of a two-story building suddenly appeared behind her. Its massive lights shone down on her as she got back on her feet and threw what looked like several grenades or bombs toward the ugly metal thing. But the tiny explosives had little impact on the machine. I remembered this girl. I had seen her before when she shot and killed someone. It was me.

The scene was captivating. It was hard for me to look away as she continued to fire her weapon at the machine and then slowly turned and, with a trained eye, looked through the scope and fired several more rounds.

The sound of deep laughter echoed through the room, causing my anger to ignite. "You look envious."

"How do you know me?" My voice rose with the last word.

"What do you see about her that makes you think it's you?"

"The way she walks and looks. She reminds me of Samuel," I said.

"What else?"

"She has a pony tail with a perfect part straight down the middle." I stared intently at the image. I seemed so young in this vision. Too young to be a soldier. Why in the world would I be considered a soldier when I didn't even look old enough to drive a car?

"That's right. Why is it a perfect part?" The voice continued to push me.

"Because I like my lines straight," I responded, throwing my hands into the air in frustration. "I like perfect lines. What are you trying to tell me?"

"Exactly. You like perfection, Captain Esa James. That's one of the reasons you were such a good soldier and leader. But we have found that lines are not always perfect. Lines bend. Just like time."

"What does that mean?" I yelled. "Tell me!"

"It means, everything you have learned up until now may not be all that it seems."

"Like what?" I asked, looking up at the ceiling.

"Like this so-called 'Hunter' that has been stalking you."

"How do you know I call it the Hunter?" I wanted to understand how this voice knew so much about me. It was as if it had heard all of my thoughts over the past few years.

"Just remember, I'm always watching. You're too valuable a soldier for me to not track."

Her words made me uneasy. Too many people always had eyes on me, yet I'd somehow managed to disappear for three years. Was that really possible?

"Fine. Then why don't you tell me who it is?"

"Because, up until now, you haven't asked."

It felt like this voice was taunting me, which only frustrated me more. I didn't feel like playing games right now. I wanted answers, and I wanted to find the rest of my team.

I looked up at the ceiling again. It was another white wall, but I sensed that, somewhere up there, the voice was looking down at me. Through gritted teeth, I finally asked, "Who is it?"

The voice didn't hesitate. "Captain Esa James, its Luther, and he's become quite powerful. I think he plans to kill you and the rest of the team, but he can't kill you yet. I won't let him."

"How do you know anything about Luther?"

"I've been watching him as well." The voice made a loud sigh.

"That's impossible. We've been trying to find him, but we can't nail down the year," I said.

"You are not as good as I am."

"Who are you? Tell me who you are!"

Silence.

"Who are you?!" I yelled again, and clenched my fists.

Silence.

"You said the reason Luther hasn't killed me is because of you. What does that mean?"

Silence.

A large white door at the far end of the room slowly slid up. A flash of light blinded me momentarily as a figure walked through the door toward me.

My breath caught.

Every emotion possible rushed through me. This couldn't be happening. I wasn't prepared. I wasn't ready. I had thought so many times about what I would say when I came face to face with her. Now the moment had arrived; my mother was standing in front of me.

There was no doubt it was my mom. She was the spitting image of me, only older. Her long blonde hair also had a perfect line straight down the middle.

"Hello Captain James. It's been a while since we've talked face to face," she said in a silky smooth voice. A soft glow traced the exterior of her body.

"Yes, it's been a long time."

"Do you know who I am?" she asked, but I knew she already knew the answer.

"I assume you are my mother." My voice grew cold. This was the woman who had something to do with my disappearance. I had been back for weeks and only now was she making her existence known.

She stared into my eyes as if she could read my thoughts and then she slowly nodded. "That's correct."

"You are the reason I disappeared for three years." I folded my arms over my chest defiantly, willing her to say something that would make me care about her.

"Esa, you are my daughter, but you are also a soldier. Sometimes we have to do things for the greater good."

"The wha—?"

She abruptly raised her hand. "Shh. You heard me—the greater good. Now you have found me, and it's time we start planning for the next wave."

"Stop. What are you talking about?"

"Luther is hunting you. He intends to kill you and me," she responded nonchalantly.

"Why does he hate me so much?" It was a question that had haunted me for a while. There was so much hatred in the way Luther had talked to me several weeks ago. He had shown me what had happened to his body when he had gone on the Jump Line too early, but that wasn't my fault. There had to be more to it.

"He already told you. It's because of me. You are my daughter and my top soldier. Luther could never be as good as you and Samuel. He was a second-class recruit, and I told him so, but it doesn't really matter now. Troy and Paul found their weak link and they've been using Luther since he first showed any sign of no longer wanting to be part of the team."

"Paul and Troy?" I whispered. "Is Paul also using Luther?"

"Yes. You still have a lot more to learn. Now, follow me."

My mother turned and strode out the door. I waited several seconds and then followed. I could have left, but I felt drawn to see where she was going and what information she might be able to provide. There were too many unanswered questions swirling around in my head. She had mentioned Paul.

A bright white light suddenly blinded me.

I blinked several times. I was lying down on something. My body was definitely no longer in an upright position. What was happening?

I frantically tried to review my surroundings. The bright light above made it hard for me to see anything, but I knew I was no longer inside the massive room. I reached up and tried to push the light away, but my limbs felt like limp noodles. Every time I raised my arm, it fell back onto the table with a loud thud.

Images of me lying on a table suddenly overtook my thoughts. I could see myself. I could see the fear in my eyes.

I tried to lift my right arm, then my left. Nothing. They lay lifeless next to my body. Nothing seemed to work. My mind was quickly becoming clearer, but it was as if I were trapped inside my body. As a full wave of panic began to set in, Paul's face came into view.

"Good morning, my child. How are you feeling?"

Paul? What was he doing here? I tried to respond, but I couldn't seem to form the words. Instead, only a series of odd sounds and grunts came from my mouth.

"I see the medicine still hasn't worn off. Go back to sleep. You will be fine in a few hours."

His face left my view, and I could feel my eyes grow heavy. I didn't want to sleep right now. I wanted to be awake. I wanted to talk with my mother some more. She had told me to follow her, but now I was here with Paul. Something was happening. I needed to stay awake, but I couldn't help it. My eyelids were growing heavier with each breath.

No, no, no. Don't fall asleep, I tried to will myself. Fight, Esa. Fight.

It was no use.

My mother had said something about Paul and Troy working together. I had to remember more about what she had told me, but the medicine was too strong and I was too weak.

Chapter Nine

C hapter Nine

"Esa, Esa, wake up," a hushed voice said somewhere in the distance. This time the voice was familiar. My body shook back and forth as she once again whispered frantically into my ear. "Esa, you need to wake up." This time there was definitely a sense of urgency and maybe a little bit of fear in her tone.

I tried to say something in response, but my mouth felt dry, like a dozen cotton balls had been stuffed inside and were sitting there scratching the back of my throat.

A cool liquid suddenly touched my lips. Water! Someone was pouring water into my mouth. The crisp coolness felt good on my tongue. I tried to lick up more.

"Esa, wake up! We have to go," the voice said again, closer to my ear. I tried to silently encourage my heavy eyelids to open. Finally, I felt the first, and then the second, lift slightly, only to be greeted by darkness. I blinked several times. Someone was standing in front of me, but it was hard to make out who it was. Everything was so fuzzy.

After several seconds, her face came into full view. It was Audrina.

I coughed, trying to clear my throat.

Audrina kept staring back at me, saying something. Her lips were definitely moving, but I couldn't hear any sounds. She must have gone ahead and put us on the Jump Line. I could feel its energy and then we were somewhere else. The air was warmer and I could feel the sun on my face.

I began to shake my head again trying to clear away all of the fuziness and then she did it...she slapped me across the face.

"Esa, wake up. Seriously, you've got to open up your eyes." I heard her say again, her voice going up a few octaves. I wanted to let her know that I was trying. Audrina had to know that I wasn't ignoring her pleas. I wanted to be awake as well, but it didn't feel like my brain was talking to the rest of my body.

I tried to lift my hand again. This time, I could feel a slight movement. I tried again and, to my surprise, my right hand rose high enough for me to see it.

"That's good, Esa. Do it again. Next time, I'll help pull you up."

I nodded and willed myself to raise my hand again. She grabbed ahold of my fingers and pulled me upright. I tried to force myself to not fall back.

My muscles ached from the movement. I rolled my wrist several times, trying to start the process of getting my body back to normal. I sat in the upright position for several seconds taking in the view in front of me.

"Audrina, where are we?" I finally managed to get out. My voice sounded more hoarse than normal.

"We're in the year 2005, but we were just inside of OnyxFive," she shook her head. "I tried to wake you up, but it was no use. Finally, I just made the jump. We had to get out of there. I'm surprised I even had enough time to get you water. Paul has been in the room non-stop."

"Where are the others?" I asked, still unsure of the situation. How did I know it was really Audrina this time? "Where is the rest of the team?"

"I don't know."

We sat in silence for several seconds as we both tried to collect our thoughts. The sight in front of us was beautiful, magical. The outside air felt welcoming on my skin. Slowly, my body was beginning to wake. I could easily move my arms and legs again. My mouth still felt dry, but it was better than it had been back at OnyxFive.

I looked over at Audrina. "Is this real?"

A tear rolled down her cheek. "What does that mean? Why are you asking if this is real?"

"I'm sorry. I just need to know."

"Esa, it's me, Audrina." She held up her arm and pinched the skin, as if to prove that it was really her.

My head was spinning. "Thank you. I'm sorry. So much has happened lately, I'm not sure what to think or who to trust."

"I know. Me either. I had some really weird dreams. They were very real and my head still feels a fuzzy. The medicine must be our systems."

"What medicine?"

"Paul drugged us. He somehow managed to capture the two of us and he started doing a series of tests."

"What sort of tests?"

"I'm not sure." She shook her head vigorously.

"Have you seen Samuel, Theo or Gave since the hallway?" I glanced around at the meadow, wondering if the boys were somewhere near us.

"No. I don't know where they are right now. I woke several times while we were under and heard Paul murmuring unhappily about us, saying that we weren't listening to his orders. I remember seeing you hooked up to a weird-looking machine. You had tubes coming out of your mouth, hands and feet. It really freaked me out, but there wasn't anything I could do. The medicine was too strong and it put me back to sleep. At some point, my head cleared and I saw you lying on the table next to me. The tubes were gone."

More tears flowed down Audrina's cheeks. Her sobs became uncontrollable as her body shook. She seemed so different right now. Much more vulnerable than the Audrina I had come to know over the past few weeks. "Esa, Paul grabbed us in the hallway. I don't know what happened to the others. I don't know what's going on, but I would love to find some answers."

"I don't know either," I whispered, trying to mentally put the puzzle pieces together as I gazed down at my hands, wondering what sort of tubes Paul had connected me to, but everything looked normal now. "But I intend to find out too."

"We need some sort of plan," she stared out at the flowers.

I nodded, hoping I looked more confident than I felt. My mind went back to the moment we were walking behind the soldiers in the hallway. The Hunter had been there and had started shooting. One of Paul's guards had been hit and killed. I remembered watching his body fall to the floor. After that, everything had happened so fast.

"Audrina, what do you recall from the hallway?" I tugged at a strand of my hair.

"I remember feeling the same rush of energy inside my body as I felt when whatever that thing was pushed me into the water."

"Did it come on suddenly?" I rubbed my arms, thinking back to when I had first felt the Hunter's presence in the hallway at OnyxFive.

"Yes. I could feel the energy from the team, but then suddenly there was another source—a stronger source—and it was coming toward us at a fast pace and then it stopped near us. It was very close to me."

I nodded in agreement. "That's what I felt too. That thing was back, but this time it managed to grab one of the guard's guns."

She looked over at me, suspicion etched into her features. "Esa, what was it? Was it something Paul created to attack us?"

"It's not a what; it's who," I dropped my head into my hands, thinking back to the conversation I'd had with my mother. Had it even been real? It had felt like it had been. She'd seemed very human.

"Well then, who is it?" Audrina asked. I could tell she was eager to have some sort of answer. This had been as hard for her as it had for me. The look in her eyes told me what I needed to know—we were both real. This moment was real. Audrina was sitting next to me. This time, she wasn't going to disappear into thin air.

At first, I couldn't get the words to leave my mouth. I wanted to tell her, but there was something that seemed to stop me from uttering anything. Finally, I managed to whisper, "It's Luther."

Her eyes burned with anger at the sound of his name. "What does that traitor want now?" She seethed, clenching her fists. "I swear, I'll kill him.

He has ruined everything for us. I just want to wrap my hands around his throat and electrocute him. I know my guy in the tunnel would definitely take Luther's body for a trade."

"We can't trade his body. We're not sure exactly what they would be able to pull from it. Aud, I agree about Luther ruining everything, but we don't know where he is or what he's done to make himself invisible. He obviously had some help, and I don't think he got that help from Troy."

"Hmm. Then we need to go on our own hunt," Audrina said, standing and swiping at several random pieces of dirt on the front of her white outfit. "Let's go find the traitor. This time, we will find him and kill him before he is able to come after us."

"Yes!"

Standing next to her, I had a sense of purpose. I was tired of being attacked by Luther, Paul and whoever else decided they wanted to capture our team.

"I agree with the plan, but before we kill him, we need to get Luther to tell us who he's working with right now. Is it just Troy, or is Paul somehow involved? After he talks, then we can decide how we want to dispose of him."

Chapter Ten

- -

C hapter Ten

"Esa, do you suddenly feel a little weird?" Audrina's eyes narrowed. Her face had started to contort into an odd look. The excitement from only seconds ago had quickly worn off.

"What do you mean? Are you asking if I feel weird because I'm sitting in the middle of a field of flowers with you?" I responded, unsure of exactly what was going on right now, but suddenly scared Audrina might disappear on me again.

Too many things had happened recently. Of course I felt weird. Everything seemed off right now.

She shook her head. "I know what you're thinking, but what I'm feeling is different. I suddenly don't feel right. I can't explain it. It's like all of the electricity has left my body. I can't feel it anymore." She held out her hand and turned her palm upward. It was empty. There was nothing inside. Her eyes widened as she turned back to me. "Oh my God. Did you see that? What's happening, Esa?"

Flashes of the scene from when I was in the massive room came rushing back. Audrina had disappeared in front of my eyes. She hadn't been real. Was that about to happen again? Was her body going to dissolve into tiny speckles?

Things are not always as they seem.

Those words echoed through my thoughts.

"Esa, that scene you were just thinking about...where was it?"

My gaze snapped over to her and my eyes narrowed. "What do you mean? What scene?"

"I saw what you were thinking about just now. I saw Samuel and then me. I disappeared in front of you. Oh my God. Oh my God, Esa. What's going on?" She clenched her fists. "This is all too much. I swear, I just want to hurt someone right now. I hate all of these games."

Flashes of Audrina running through OnyxFive with a loaded weapon and firing the gun at Paul and his guards filled my mind.

Oh my God, now I was reading her thoughts. The idea stopped me cold. How was it possible for us to suddenly read each other's minds?

"Audrina, I think the medicine Paul gave us has altered our systems. He's changing us."

"What? Why?!" she shrieked. "Why would he want to change us? I like the way we are, and I never consented to being altered." Audrina's frown deepened into a full scowl. "I knew we shouldn't have trusted him. I told Samuel so that day he brought him to Mary's cabin. Over the years, I have told your brother repeatedly not to get too close to Paul, but he never listens. Samuel wants so badly to have his family back, that he compromised the entire team."

I raised my hands. "Stop. This isn't about Samuel."

We were still in the middle of the field. Everything seemed so calm and peaceful, except for what was happening in our thoughts. We both were thinking back to the scene in the hallway, and the way Paul had looked.

A flock of large white birds flew overhead. This is how the world should be, I thought. It should be full of color and life, not darkness.

"I like the birds too," Audrina meekly replied. "I'm sorry, Esa. I'm trying to figure out all of the emotions I'm currently feeling. I'm angry and for one of the first times in my life, I'm scared. I also miss Samuel right now. We need him and the rest of the team."

"I know," I responded, thinking about Theo and Gave. "We also need to stop feeling sorry for ourselves. The boys would not be happy if they knew we were sitting in a meadow crying."

A soft smile pulled at the corners of Audrina's lips. "You're right. Sorry. I just had an off moment."

"I know, but now we've got to start thinking about our next move."

"Esa, hold out your palm," she said, holding out her own again. I knew she was probably secretly hoping to see some sign of electricity.

I held out my hand, but there was nothing. I shook my head. "I can't feel anything either. The electricity is gone. You were right."

The last sentence hung in the air.

She grabbed my wrist. "So neither of us have any electricity? Esa, we are easy targets if we don't have any way to fight off our attackers. We need to get our hands on some weapons. I know where we can get some."

"Okay." I said, pulling my hand away from hers. Audrina's nails had left little indentions on my wrist.

The thought that our bodies were changing was fully setting in for me. I may have lost my memory prior to three years ago, but the one thing I had always been sure about was that I had a way to protect myself.

"This doesn't seem possible. How are we suddenly so different? Are you sure it's not something about this place?"

"We jumped to thirty years before our primary year. There's nothing unusual about this year. Trust me, I've made this jump many times. That's why we landed here. This is the place I come to when I need to get away and think. Samuel also comes here often."

I bit down on my lip. "It's beautiful. I can see why you both like it."

There was little doubt as to why Audrina had chosen this spot in this time. It was peaceful and full of color—a nice escape from the darkness of our current world.

"Esa, I was in this spot when that thing found me and took me under the water," she said, pointing off into the distance. Usually I stay right here, but that day I'd realized there is a large lake on the other side of that ridge. I didn't have a chance to get a good look because I was being pushed down into the darkness."

I could suddenly see Audrina standing in the middle of the meadow, and her body being lifted by something, moved over to the cliff, and thrown into the dark water. I could feel her fear as her body was pushed farther and farther toward the bottom. It was dark and cold. She tried to scream, but the water filled her mouth. The Hunter had a tight grip on her and wasn't going to let her go. Then an image of Gave came out of nowhere. He was swimming frantically toward Audrina. When he finally got close enough, he grabbed her hand and pulled her back toward the surface. The Hunter was gone.

I shook my head to clear my thoughts. "Gave had said he was able to see you."

"That's just what I was thinking about. Gave found me in the water."

"I don't know what's happening, but we need to be on our guard. I don't know how we would feel the Hunter if it came back. We're too vulnerable right now."

"What's the 'Hunter'?"

"It's the thing you were just talking about. I call it the Hunter, since obviously it is hunting us."

"But I thought it was Luther." Her eyes searched mine, waiting for my answer.

"It is. At least, that's who I think it is," I responded, lost in my own thoughts.

"We should just call it Luther instead of the Hunter. That makes me hate him more." Anger ignited in her eyes.

"Okay." I thought about the last time I had come face to face with Luther. His eyes had seemed so cold and distant.

"Esa!" Audrina hit my shoulder. "Stop thinking about him. I don't want to see his face."

I couldn't help but let out a soft chuckle. "Hmm. Then why don't you stop reading my mind?"

"Trust me. Right now, I wish I could, but for some reason I can't seem to turn it off."

She also began to laugh. "Crap. What are we going to do?"

"I'm not quite sure yet, but we'll figure it out. I think we first need to find the others."

She wrapped her arm around the back of my shoulders. "We do need them. They annoy me, but right now I wish they were here with us."

"Me too." It was true. I wished that all three of them were with me and Audrina in the field. Maybe one of them would know what to do.

That's when it hit me.

"Audrina, where else did you and Samuel visit? Think about spots you might not have mentioned to anyone else. Maybe he's hidden something for us—some sort of clue so that we can find him without having to go back to OnyxFive. He did that for me once before."

A smile danced across her face and she softly bit down on one side of her lip. "Good point. Samuel is too smart not to have planned ahead."

"Let's go find him."

"Yes, let's go find him. It will be like a scavenger hunt."

"Sure," I said. "Hopefully, that's what it will be."

Chapter Eleven

C hapter Eleven

There are points in life when you have to pause and wonder why you are the one experiencing them right at that moment in time. Ha! Time. Such an important word, but something that can be so subjective. What is time?

A soft breeze wafted through the field, blowing the flowers' long stems back and forth as Audrina and I continued to plan our next move. I told her more about talking with my mother. She agreed that Dr. Marie James seemed too real to be a dream, a figment of my imagination, or even a ghost.

Our plan included first finding Samuel and the rest of the team. Then my mother. She was somewhere, and I now felt, she was probably closer than we had ever thought.

Audrina looked over at me. "There is a place Samuel and I have been working on for the past few years. No one on the team knows about it, so it should be safe. Shall we go there?"

"Where is it?" I could see a vast area of white in her thoughts. It looked like snow.

"Hold on," Audrina said as she stood.

Before I could utter another word, she grabbed my hand and we were both on the Jump Line.

In a flash, the soft vapors of the line disappeared and we were standing inside some sort of cave, with large icicles hanging down from the ceiling. I took a deep breath. The cold air stung my lungs.

"Where are we?" A cloud of steam left my mouth with each word.

"We are up in the Northern Sector, in a place now known as Quadrant One."

"I've never heard of any place called Quadrant One."

"It started a few years ago, when we were looking for you. The war was slowly destroying all the land. Samuel knew we needed another way to identify certain areas of the planet, so he divided them up into Quadrants. It allowed us to be more strategic on where we had been and where we were going, as well as where we had spotted normals or soldiers."

"Okay, why did you visit here?"

"Because of the cold. We couldn't be tracked up here. We found our signal was too weak. It became the perfect hiding spot when we wanted to get away from the rest of the team." A sly smile tugged at the corners of her mouth. Then she turned and headed farther back into the cave.

Large sheets of ice covered part of the floor, making it difficult to walk down the narrow pathway. I could feel my bottom lip shiver from the cold.

"A few more steps, Esa. I promise, you will be warm soon."

Suddenly, the cave opened up into a large room with a bright blue pool of water in the center. Somewhere near the top of the cavern, a section of rock was missing, allowing natural light to fill the area.

"Wow, it's beautiful," I said, staring at the blue abyss that lay below us. The water was crystal clear and perfectly still.

"I know. It is amazing. It's also freezing cold, so don't fall in, because I am not going after you," Audrina said in a distant voice. She continued to walk several steps ahead.

My teeth chattered even more. "Are we almost there? I'm not sure how much more of the cold my body can take."

"Come over here, Esa," Audrina said, turning into another smaller cave.

After three or four steps we reached a large steel door. She swiped her hand in the air and a small screen appeared. A pale light shone onto Audrina's face. It looked like some sort of facial recognition device. A moment later, the lock clicked open.

Audrina pulled open the door and we stumbled inside, trying to get out of the cold. I wasn't sure what to expect on the other side, but for some reason, I knew I could trust Audrina. We were in this together. She was my teammate, my family.

One by one, lights illuminated the space.

"Hold on, Esa. Give it a few seconds," she said, walking off.

Several large couches were set in the middle of the room, alongside a long table that instantly turned into a fire pit.

"What is this place?" I continued to look around as I crossed to the fire. It felt good to hold my hands up to the hot flames.

"Samuel and I started to build it two years ago. He knew our place would eventually be compromised and he wanted to have a back-up. Slowly, and very quietly, we began acquiring stuff to make it a fully functional space. I think Samuel knew it was someone on the team who was providing information to Troy. He didn't want to trust anyone. We have been calling it Station One, but really it could go by any name."

"This place is amazing." I stood in awe at the idea that they had planned something so elaborate. "Station One. Okay."

"I know. It has been fun sneaking away to come here, undetected."

A screen on the far wall came to life, and a familiar robot came into view.

"Good to see you arrived safely. I am bringing up the interior temperature."

"LUX?" I said, surprised to see her.

Audrina laughed. "It's not LUX. This is a different version. Esa, meet LUX-2. She looks similar to the previous version, so that, when we need her, no one will be able to tell the difference, but Samuel knows how to tell if it's LUX or this model."

LUX-2 looked back at both of us, expressionless. "Captain Samuel James asked me to make him aware of your arrival. Do I have your permission to send him the alert?"

Audrina stopped in her tracks. "LUX-2, was he operating in distress when he asked you to make that request? Was Paul with him?"

"Yes, General Lyons was standing beside him."

"Okay. That's what I thought." Audrina glanced over at me and shook her head before turning back to the screen. "LUX-2, I'm sorry, but please go ahead and self-destruct."

"I understand. Three...two...one." LUX-2's screen went dark. As did the rest of the compound.

"Wait! What are you doing, Audrina? We need her."

"Esa, we've been compromised. Paul has probably already tried to hack into the system. We can't afford for him to find some way to trace any message LUX-2 might send. But Samuel will get a notification that 'LUX' is not operating. Trust me, he will know what that means. We've discussed this before. He and I are the only two who can make LUX, or LUX-2, become inoperable. He will know we are here."

"Okay, but do we have any other sort of computer system here that can operate this place?" I asked. "We won't have much time here if we can't turn the heater back on."

"Esa, get a grip," she said, her shoulder brushing mine as she moved. "We had no choice. If Paul finds us here, I'm out of options. This is the one place Samuel created so we could possibly be safe...and survive. Things are a little different now that Paul knows how to get on the Jump Line. We have to be extra cautious. Besides, Samuel will be able to reprogram a new variation of her at some point. We also have a special generator."

Just as the last word escaped her mouth, the lights and fire pit turned back on.

"Thank you," I said, looking around the, once again, well-lit structure.

I turned to the right just in time to see Samuel appear in the room, a serious look on his face. "Where have you guys been?"

Audrina let out a squeal of delight. "You made it! You figured out my message! I knew you would!"

"Yes, but where have the two of you been?" He strode over to me and Audrina, and as he drew closer, his expression turned into a scowl.

"Paul had us. He was running some sort of experiments," Audrina responded. She tried to wrap her arms around Samuel's neck, but he pulled away from her grasp.

"It's been over a month since we were attacked in the hallway. Are you telling me you've both been at OnyxFive since then and we couldn't find you inside the facility?" There was a questioning look on his face. It was almost as if he didn't believe us.

Both of our mouths dropped open.

"A month?" I asked. It didn't seem possible. The hallway attack had just happened; at least, that's how it seemed. Audrina and I hadn't been gone that long. I looked over at my brother. "There's no way we have been gone for a month. It feels like everything just happened the other day."

"It's been a month. Trust me," Samuel responded in a dry tone. "One very long month. Theo, Gave and I were able to get out and have been searching for both you ever since, but we couldn't track either of you. It was like when Esa disappeared the first time, only now it was both of you gone without a trace."

I held out my palm. "Paul did something to the electricity inside of our bodies. He's changing us."

Samuel rubbed his chin as he stared down at my hand. "Hmm. I'm obviously missing something. Why would he be altering your physical make-up?"

"He must be getting ready for something and hasn't fully told us his plans," I responded, looking back at him.

"Good point. Paul has obviously not been very truthful lately, and I intend to find out what is going on." He placed his hands on his hips. "He swore to me that he just wanted to do some standard testing on us, and that he hadn't intended what happened in the hallway...and I believed him."

"Where are the others?" Audrina asked, glancing over at the empty couch. It was almost as if she expected Theo and Gave to appear at any moment.

"I didn't tell them I thought I had found you. They are not aware of this place yet. We've been jumping through time non-stop trying to figure out what's going on, but the past few weeks have provided us with very little information. I guess it's time for me to get them and bring them here so we can discuss what we need to do next."

"Has the Hunter returned?" I asked Samuel.

"What are you talking about?" Samuel's eyebrows creased.

"The invisible thing that keeps attacking us."

"Oh. Got it. Yes, Gave and Theo have both had nasty run-ins with this so-called Hunter. Theo, thankfully, gave it a nice beating. We haven't seen it for the past week."

"What if it's waiting for you to bring Theo and Gave here so it can follow and attack all of us?"

"That could happen, but we can't fight or plan if we don't have the entire team, and now that you've mentioned OnyxFive, I want to make sure we steer clear of that place. It's no longer safe for us to be around Paul. Give me a few seconds; I'll be right back." Samuel disappeared.

Almost instantly, he returned with Theo and Gave by his side. Theo blinked several times when he saw Audrina and me standing off to the side of the room.

Before I could utter a word, he hastened toward me. He paused for several seconds, staring into my eyes. I could see anger and hurt. He must have thought I had disappeared again for good.

"Where have you guys been?" he demanded.

"Paul apparently had them," Samuel responded for us. "I'm really sorry, guys. I thought things had changed and I could trust him."

"I'm going to kill him." Theo seethed.

"I agree. We can in time, but not yet," Samuel said. "We need to focus on other things first."

Chapter Twelve

C hapter Twelve

"Where are we?" Theo looked around the small room. "What is this place?"

"Welcome to Station One," Audrina said. "We should be safe here for a little while."

"I don't get it. How did you guys find this place?" Theo asked.

"We didn't just find it. We built it," Samuel responded. "Too many things were happening for us not to have a back-up plan in place. This is one of those plans."

I caught what he had just said. "So, there are more places like this one in existence?"

"Maybe." Samuel glanced at Audrina. "But I'm not ready to disclose those locations. We should be safe here. I don't think Luther ever figured out that this place existed. I also don't think Paul knows anything about Station One. We should be good."

"You may need to reprogram LUX-2 if you want us to stay here. She's not operating," I said.

"Good point. That shouldn't take me too long. She's on a different system than LUX."

"Wait! There are two LUXs?" Gave asked.

"There were, but we just ordered the second one to self-destruct," I responded.

"Don't worry. We have a structure in place to handle the reprogramming of any LUX robot. Esa and Audrina, I want to get a download from both of you about what has happened over the past few weeks, but for now, follow me," Samuel said, walking out of the room, not waiting on any of us. He turned and poked his head back in briefly. "Seriously. Come on, guys. We don't have time to waste just staring at one another."

We all watched as Samuel waved his hand forward in an effort to get us all to follow. Several of the team looked unsure. Audrina was the first to take a few steps.

"We should follow him," she said, motioning for us to get in line behind her. "Otherwise, he's just going to come right back and pull you along with him."

The four of us walked down a small hallway that turned into a larger, circular room.

"Oh my God. It's your lab." The room was an exact replica of his old lab, with large computer screens covering the walls.

"Yes. I like this layout, but what I really wanted to show you is what I came across once I finally had access to Troy's files," he said, waving his hand into the empty space in front of us. A holographic image appeared, showing several small circular buildings.

"What is it?" I asked, trying to make out the individual images.

"We were right about him finding a new planet, but we had some of the details wrong. It's what he had originally called 'Project Sapien,' but is now being called Merak. It has everything we need to survive: land, a good atmosphere. Look at some of the pictures of the plant life. It's thriving. Troy was able to get additional images to see if there was any humanoid life on the planet, but it looks like there's only some animals."

"If he's found a place then why does he need us?"

"It's a long flight to Merak. Two years ago, he sent up a ship with twenty-five normals, but they won't arrive for at least another year. He thinks we could make the trip on the Jump Line. I think he has been having Luther practice."

"Are these normals ones who should still be living in another time?" I asked. Troy and Luther had been kidnapping perfectly healthy normals from a variety of years and holding them for his mission to this new place. Most of the normals had special skill sets. Unfortunately, Troy was forgetting that his actions would eventually have very serious consequences. Ripples in time had to be happening because he had taken so many people.

"Yes," Samuel responded. "It's a lot more than we thought. I'm really surprised we haven't seen more changes in the timeline."

"We haven't exactly been looking for the changes. They may be happening, and we just aren't aware because we're so far removed," Audrina said. "I mean, look at us. We've been so busy searching for Luther and Troy, we haven't been paying attention to what's going on around us."

"You've also been gone for a month," Theo said.

"What about the normals living in the tunnels? Have any of you made runs to get them food and supplies?" she asked.

"Yes," Theo answered. "We made a run the other day. It's been quiet down there. They must know something is up. I would definitely warn that we need to be more cautious when we go down there right now."

I hadn't thought about it, but Audrina was right. Our team had been bringing back food and plants for a number of factions, but our missions had definitely declined since we'd moved into OnyxFive.

"That's true," Samuel said. "It has been a lot quieter in the tunnels. We've only had a few orders. I agree. It should make us nervous."

Theo cleared his throat. "We have to find Luther and Troy and stop them from taking any more healthy normals. It's already too many. We also need to figure out what we've been missing for the past two months."

"Do you think our mission to hunt down Luther and Troy was just a ruse? Maybe Paul put us up to it to make sure we were distracted, while something else was going on in the background," I said, thinking back to the last time I had walked the perimeter of OnyxFive and Paul had called me back in after only a few minutes.

Samuel shook his head. "That's what I've been wondering, and I have a feeling that the answer is probably yes. I'm sorry, guys. It's my fault."

"Where is this new planet?" I walked around the image in front of me, not giving Samuel any additional time to wallow.

Samuel scrolled through some of the images of the normals who had been selected for Troy's test flight. They were all ages, ethnicities, genders.

"At least Troy was smart enough to diversify and make sure to get both men and women," I stared intently at the pictures.

"Yeah, but I think that's just luck. If you look at the notes, all of these people have pretty remarkable backgrounds. There is everything from Olympic athletes to medical doctors, to chefs. One of the people in the group is even a famous architect," Audrina said. "The abduction of these normals will not go unnoticed."

"From what I can tell from Troy's maps, Merak is just outside of our solar system," Samuel said. "I'm really not sure how he found the place. I don't know if we could make the trip on the Jump Line, but it's definitely worth the try."

"I wonder what he is going to tell all of these people when they wake up on a new planet, in a new year," Gave said. "It must be very confusing."

"What else have you seen?" I asked.

"Troy has dozens of digital images stored on his computer. The normals we found at NorthStar haven't made the trip yet. I found the timeline for the next ship to be launched. The date has already passed, so I'm not sure if a new one has been set. There has been no movement on Troy's hard drive for the past month. He must know we are onto him and has found a new way to work."

"What about Troy? Has he been to Merak?" Theo asked. He folded his hands behind his head as he continued to stare at the images.

"No. I don't believe he's ever made the trip. At least, it doesn't seem possible, but there's no doubt in my mind, he is working on a transportation mechanism right now to resume the trips. I have a feeling he's also started to replicate Luther, or he's created a new variation of Luther. We knew that was only a matter of time now that Troy is being rushed."

"How does Paul factor into this?" I asked, staring at Samuel.

Samuel looked over at me, confused. "What do you mean? Paul and Troy are on different sides of the fight."

"They may have been on opposite sides at one point, but they've become unified. I found out that Paul and Troy are working together." I took a big gulp of air as the last few words slid out of my mouth. They would all surely ask me for an explanation, and then I would have to tell them what I had seen and experienced in the large white room.

"How do you know that?" His eyes narrowed.

I looked around at the rest of the team. Audrina nodded, giving me the confidence to continue on with my story.

"I saw our mother. She told me."

Samuel's eyes widened. "You did? You saw her while you were at OnyxFive? That doesn't make sense."

"Yes and no. She came to me in a dream after the ambush in the hallway. I thought she was the one who helped me escape the attack. It was only later that I found out from Audrina that we had been at OnyxFive the whole time. It was really weird. She was standing in the middle of a large room. Samuel, you were right...she's alive."

Samuel turned back to the image. "I don't understand."

"Samuel, it's too coincidental that she has visited us both. She seemed too real in the dream to be a ghost or a figment of my imagination."

"Esa, did she give you any idea on how to find her?"

"No, but we were in a place with ice. Kind of like this place. How did you discover this location?"

Samuel paused and then shrugged his shoulders. "I've never really thought about it, but I guess it's because she led me here. She planted the seed in me that building something in colder temperatures would help us hide. I started looking for a good site and this one kept coming up on my system."

"Do you think she might be closer than we think?" A wave of hope washed over me. Was it possible that my mother was close by?

"I don't know. I've often thought about it, but I really haven't had the time to go and search for her. I was too busy finding you, and trying to keep the team one step ahead of Troy...and, I guess, Paul. Though I'm still not convinced the two are working together."

Gave cleared his throat. "Don't forget, it was Paul who had the armed guards come and get us, and apparently it was Paul who was holding Audrina and Esa for the past month."

"True," said Samuel, nodding. "I knew something was up at that time, but I thought he was working a different angle. Maybe trying to show his team he could still be trusted."

A slow rumble somewhere outside of building caused the floor to shake. I tightened my grip on the table in front of me. Theo also walked towards the object that seemed to be affixed to the floor.

Samuel laughed. "Don't worry about that. It happens. The ground is a little unstable up here, but at least it's a place where we can prepare for the next fight. Paul shouldn't be able to find us up here. The cold messes with anyone being able to feel the energy emitted from our bodies."

"Now we just need to figure out a plan. Who do we go after first? Do we split up or stay together?" Audrina crossed her arms over her chest as her eyes slowly moved from each one of us while she waited for a response.

"We know there's something in 1965 that Luther keeps going to, but we haven't been able to find him," Theo said.

"Maybe we haven't been able to catch him because he's altered his genetic make-up and is no longer visible to the human eye," I said, thinking back to the invisible thing that had attacked me.

"If it is Luther who has been attacking us, then Troy has definitely done something to him. I didn't realize Troy had those skills. He's an astrophysicist, not a medical doctor," Theo responded. "Unless he is getting help from someone."

"He has to have help. Someone has been mapping Luther's genetic code and making changes. I assume it's so he can create the right type of soldier to travel and survive Merak. Think about it. Luther was able to push you down into the depths of the water." Samuel looked over at Audrina. "Theo's right. He's become strong. A lot stronger than he was before."

Audrina turned toward Gave. "But then you saw me. Esa and I had something similar happen to us a little while ago. We were able to read each other's minds."

Theo crossed to one of the couches and sat down. "Samuel and I had the same thing happen."

"Yeah, I'm not sure I want to read Theo's mind," Samuel said, looking over at me.

"I also don't want you to read my mind." Theo huffed.

"Do you all still have electricity in your bodies?" I asked.

"Yes," Samuel said, holding out his hand. A thin blue line of electricity danced in his palm. A wave of jealousy washed over me. I hadn't expected to feel that way, but why didn't Audrina and I still have electricity? It didn't seem fair.

"Well, I guess that makes me feel a little better." I tried not to let my voice show my true feelings. It was hard knowing that such a major change had happened to my body without my knowledge or consent.

"What are you trying to say, Esa?" Theo asked.

"Audrina and I no longer have any electricity." I held out my hand. It was empty. I then held out the other. In the past, this move would have connected two sources of electricity, but now, nothing happened. "Neither of us can feel it anymore. I don't know how to explain it, but my body feels different."

"Okay," Samuel said. "I know you guys are not going to like what I have to say, but I need to test all of us. That will have a big impact on how we set a plan in motion. Then we need to figure out a way to stop Troy and find out his connection with Paul. Finally, we search for my mother."

The rest of the team began to groan at Samuel's mention of needing to run more tests. We had been through so many lately. It seemed like someone was constantly wanting to run a test on one of us.

"Our mother," I responded dryly.

"Yes, our mother, Esa. Obviously, she's somewhere, and for some reason, she doesn't want to be found. Yet, she is making her presence known. There must be a reason she is suddenly coming out of hiding." Samuel turned back to the image. "Give me a little time to think. Can you all be back in my lab in one hour?"

"I don't think we should travel on the Jump Line right now," Audrina said. "It's too risky with Paul now being able to use it."

"I agree," Samuel said without taking his eyes off of the image. "Stay here, but relax for a bit. It will give me time to calibrate my equipment."

"That's fine by me. Besides, I want to check this place out," Theo said. "Where exactly are we right now?"

"Northern Quadrant," Samuel said. "We are on an island in the Arctic Ocean."

"I've never been up here. How cold does it actually get outside?" Theo asked.

"Too cold. Station One is built inside a cave, which provides it with some protection, but if you decide to leave, you will need to be properly dressed or you will freeze before you can make it back here," Audrina said. "Make sure to cover your face and eyes. The cold will sting after only a few seconds, but really your safest bet is just to stay in the cave."

"Got it. I think I can handle a simple recon mission. Esa, do you want to go with me?"

My voice caught in my throat. Had Theo really asked me if I wanted to go exploring with him? This was something different for him. Usually, they all went on missions and made me stay behind. "Uh, yes. That sounds interesting," I said, rubbing my hands together, trying to calm my nerves. "I did get to see some of the cave already. It's really cool, but Audrina's right: it's very cold."

Audrina threw two jackets to us, along with gloves and goggles. "Wear everything and don't attempt to take anything off. Got it? We need to have the entire team intact if we are going to carry off any sort of mission to find Troy, Luther...and Paul."

"Okay," I said as we both zipped up the coats. My jacket swallowed me, covering almost my entire body. Audrina then slid over a face cover and hat.

"Esa, I know we were just out in the cold, but trust me, you will need all of this if you plan to stay outside for more than a few minutes."

"Thank you. We will be back before the hour is up," Theo said.

I looked back at the fire pit. It seemed so enticing to stay inside the warm little structure, instead of going back outside into the freezing cold.

Theo pulled open the door and a piece of ice fell at our feet. We briefly glanced at one another before stepping outside. The door closed swiftly behind us.

"Audrina and I came from that direction earlier," my voice echoed throughout the space as I pointed back toward the blue pond. Theo walked ahead of me. It was quiet, except for the sound of the wind rushing down some of the narrow walkways. After several seconds, we came to the water.

"I think we should walk around on the ledge and check out the other side," I said, pointing to the path that led around the beautiful blue pond.

"Let's go." Theo grabbed my hand. "I don't want to stand in one place for too long for fear we might freeze."

His statement made me laugh.

Theo turned back toward me. "Don't you think something is off about this place? It just seems weird that we were never told about it. How long have Samuel and Audrina been coming here?"

"She said it's been a while and that they didn't want to tell anyone on the team because they didn't know who they could trust."

"Why this place? Did she tell you that?"

"She only told me that the cold made it harder for anyone to track us. Just like Samuel said a few minutes ago. I'm assuming my mother played a bigger role, but I don't know the specifics."

"I'd sure like to know more," Theo responded.

I pulled him back. "What's going on?"

"I don't know who to trust anymore. Every time I turn around the story changes. All I know is that someone is hunting us and wants us dead, and Troy has much bigger plans that don't include this planet, and now I'm learning that Paul and Troy may be working together."

"Do you think he would intentionally cause more destruction to the planet just to get back at us?"

"I wouldn't put it past him, but really, what does it matter? In a few more weeks, the normals will no longer be able to breathe the air."

Theo slowly made his way around the narrow path that wrapped encircled the blue pool. Large icicles jutted from different areas of the low ceiling.

Just as we rounded the narrow bend, Theo's boot hit a slick patch of ice. "Esa! Watch out!" Theo said, grabbing for one of the rocks. He continued to fall backward despite my attempts to grasp his jacket.

"Theo, grab on!" I yelled, thrusting my hand toward him.

"I'm trying! I'm trying!" His arms were flailing above his head. The large pool of water loomed below him.

"Theo, you've got to take my hand or you're going to fall in!" I held onto a large rock with one hand and frantically swung out my other arm in hopes that Theo would be able to grab onto it.

Theo lunged forward, but just as our fingers brushed, he tipped backward into the water, making a large splash.

"Theo! Theo!" I yelled. "Theo! Oh my God, Theo can you hear me?"

My voice echoed through the cave. The clear blue water suddenly became active, with large spouts of water jumping out of the pool. Theo disappeared somewhere farther down.

"Theo!" I yelled again. I stayed glued in place, scanning the water for any sign of his body as Samuel, Gave and Audrina ran toward me.

"What happened?" Samuel asked, looking from me to the pool.

I shook my head, stunned. "Theo fell. He fell into the water," I said, pointing to the area where I had seen his body. The water had calmed again and looked perfectly still. It was almost eerie how quickly the water had returned to being calm.

Samuel leaned over the edge. "Are you sure? I don't see anything."

"Yes, I'm sure. I was just with him and then he slipped on an icy patch and fell in. He has to be down there somewhere. It was as if the water came alive and swallowed him up."

Audrina peered into the pool. "It doesn't look like anything has fallen into the water in the past few seconds. Look, Esa, it's as still as glass."

I stared at the pool and then scanned the rocky perimeter. "Then he's in here somewhere. We have to find him." I said, getting up and walking farther down the pathway, my eyes never leaving the water. "He has to be here," I whispered, hoping that Theo could hear me. He needed to know, I would not leave him.

Chapter Thirteen

Chapter Thirteen

"Where did he go? Please tell me where he went!" My voice was almost a full scream. Panic rushed through me and my stomach felt like a belt was being pulled tight around it. Everything seemed so surreal. "Where is he? Where is he?" I continued to mumble as I looked around at the others and then back to the water, frantically searching from top to bottom.

Audrina shook her head. "Esa, we don't know."

"You have to know. You have to know," I pleaded, hoping someone would have an answer. My world was slowly collapsing around me. Theo was gone. It had all happened so fast. One second he was walking in front of me and the next he was gone.

I looked down at the blue pool. The surface was smooth as glass. My reflection stared back at me. My white skin almost blended in with the icy background. My blue eyes had a twinge of despair. I looked pathetic.

Why had he fallen? Theo was a soldier; he knew how to recover from a bad situation.

I moved away from the ledge and leaned my head against the icy wall. The cold crept through my jacket. Tears began to sting at my eyes. I looked back at Samuel, Gave and Audrina. "Where is he? Samuel, you have to know. Where is he?"

Samuel's head fell forward. "I don't know, Esa. Can you tell us exactly happened?"

I wished I could easily put it into words, but the sad truth was, I didn't understand it myself. "We were just walking and he slipped on some ice. He should have been able to catch himself, but instead he fell into the water. The water suddenly came alive. It was unreal. Large columns of water swallowed Theo up...and then nothing."

I stood silently for several seconds, reliving the situation in my thoughts.

Audrina covered her mouth with her hand. "I saw it. I saw what Esa was talking about. The water came out of nowhere and swallowed Theo. She's telling the truth."

Suddenly, I knew what I had to do. I took off my jacket. The ledge was two steps in front of me.

"Esa, what are you doing?" Samuel asked.

"I'm going in there," I said, pointing to the blue pool.

Samuel grabbed my arm. "No!"

"You can't tell me what to do."

"Let me go."

I yanked my arm away from him and, before he could stop me, ran forward and leapt into the water. Its icy temperature stung through my jumpsuit. It felt like a thousand needles were poking every square inch of my body. The clear blue water surrounded me. Above, I could hear faint screams coming from the rest of the team.

"Esa, what do you see?" Samuel tried to yell at me, but I could only make out some of the words from beneath the surface.

I looked around under the water, but there was no sign of Theo. The large rocky surroundings of the blue pool were the only things visible...until I saw it: a small light near the bottom.

Quickly, I tried to swim toward the light. I could feel my body growing weaker from the cold. There were only seconds left before I would have to go back to the top for a breath of air. As I swam, suddenly I could see myself. I was reading Audrina's mind again. She was watching me swim toward the light. She could see what I was seeing.

Then, above me, the water began to change. It was no longer calm. The pressure altered too. My chest grew heavier the farther down I swam.

A tap on my shoulder caused me to turn. I was able to catch myself before I accidentally took in a gulp of water. Swimming above me were the other three. They had jumped in behind me. Fear began to tickle at my thoughts. All four of us were together under the cold water. We had no one to save us.

My arms were growing weaker and weaker, yet I seemed to be making little progress going toward the light.

And then, at last, we were there.

We floated outside some sort of underwater door. I raised my hand tried to touch it with my fingertips. Just as I made contact with the metal exterior, large bubbles began to surround us. The temperature of the water was changing quickly. It was getting warmer. The large door slowly rose. It led to a dark chamber. I looked back at the rest of the team. Samuel nodded and swum forward. What choice did any of us really have?

Darkness surrounded us as we entered the chamber and the door slowly slid back down. The water level inside the chamber also receded, little by little.

The four of us swam toward the top, where there were several inches of air. Our panting was the only thing audible as we waited to see what would happen next.

"Why did you guys follow me?" I gasped through deep breaths. The air felt so good in my lungs. "Now there isn't anyone left on the surface to rescue us."

"We're stronger together than we are apart. Besides, Theo is our friend. We need to find him," Samuel responded.

The water began to drain at a quicker rate. It was down to our legs and then at our ankles. We all shook in the cold air. We looked anxiously at one another, wondering what would happen next.

A moment later, another wall, opposite the door through which we'd entered, opened. A bright light filled the small chamber, causing us to raise our hands to protect our eyes from the glare. As I blinked several times, the room in front of us slowly came into view. I knew this room. I had been here before. We had found her.

Chapter Fourteen

Chapter Fourteen

"You all could have been killed," she snapped. "Are you idiots? I thought I trained you better than that." The icy look in her eyes could have cut through metal. She continued to glare at us as we stood, soaking wet and shivering, in front of her.

I defiantly met her gaze, taken aback by her tone. It felt as if she had slapped me in the face with her demeaning words. This wasn't how she had acted before, in my dream.

Every muscle in my body tightened as I tried to forget about the cold. Two could play at this game.

"We came to get Theo."

"Theo is still in recovery," she said, her expression darkening.

"What does that mean?" I huffed.

"It means exactly what I just said: he is in recovery and he will not be able to leave with you right now," she pulled out a small object from her pocket and rolled it in her hands.

Samuel stepped up behind me and rested his hand on my shoulder.

"Hello, Mother," he said in a soft voice. I could tell the encounter made him nervous; he hadn't expected her to act like this.

Her glare whipped over to his face. "Don't call me that ever again, Captain Samuel James. You are all soldiers. It's time you start acting like it."

"Then what should we call you?" Audrina asked skeptically from behind me, her voice a little shaky.

"My name is Dr. James. Welcome to Artek. Please don't get too comfortable. You won't be staying very long." She turned on her heels and strode away. Her shoes made a clack, clack, clack sound as she exited the room, leaving us cold...and alone.

Samuel's back was rigid as he stared at the door through which Dr. James had passed. His face said it all, he was shaken and disappointed.

Gave crossed his arms over his chest. Through his shivering lips he said, "Whoa! She's always been serious, but I've never seen her that angry. I definitely don't think she wanted us to find her."

"Too bad," I said, pushing past him and running toward the door. "Dr. Marie James!" I yelled down an empty hallway. My voice echoed in the quiet. "Dr. James!" I yelled again. I wasn't going to let her get away with this. She had the answers we all wanted.

"Captain Esa James, please keep your voice down. This is a science research facility," she said, walking out of another room and staring back at me. "We have a lot of important work happening here and I don't want my scientists distracted by your antics."

"I will keep my voice down, if you tell me what's going on," I said, clenching my fists. Finally, I was getting to talk with my mother, but it wasn't going the way I had hoped. I was beginning to think, dealing with her was worse than working with Paul, and he was pretty bad.

"You have compromised my work. I wasn't ready for you to come here. It's as simple as that. Now, please go into that room and get some new clothes before you freeze to death."

"But you were ready enough to plant the seed for Samuel to build something above this place." I pointed to the ceiling, but I wasn't exactly sure where Samuel's lab lay. We had swam down in the water, but I knew I was probably turned around.

"Yes, you all have lost your focus over the past few years. It was time for someone to get you back on the right path," she said nonchalantly. "But this isn't what I had planned. You should have known better."

The other three had joined me in the hallway.

"What should we have known?" Samuel asked. His lips had turned a purplish color.

"I would have come and gotten you when I was ready," Dr. James snapped. "You, of all people, Captain Samuel James, should know how to follow orders."

"What orders? You haven't been around for more than three years. You disappeared just like Esa!" he yelled at her. "You left us without anything. The team had to fend for itself."

"Wrong. I trained you to be strong enough to handle anything. I provided you with a place to hide. I watched over you and made sure you with the right clues to give you direction, and I hid some very valuable information with Esa. It's information that I would like back, since I'm not really sure I can trust you to keep it safe."

"Too bad. You're not getting it," Samuel responded defiantly. "I've looked at your research. It's very interesting."

"I know it is," she said in a smooth voice. "My work is always perfect. Now, leave."

"Just take us to Theo and we will be out of your way," I said. "That's the only reason we came here."

"He's not ready," she responded quickly. "I will send him back to you when I'm done."

"Like hell. Just let us see Theo and we will let you get back to your work," I snapped back at her.

"Tsk tsk, Captain Esa James. You are a little too predictable. Relationships can cause weakness. Don't ever get too close to anyone." She leaned down and whispered into my ear. "That was your biggest mistake." She ran her hands down her white coat in what looked like an attempt to smooth out invisible wrinkles. "Well, since you won't leave, I want to scan all of you, to make sure you haven't led Paul or Troy to my location."

"No. How can we trust you?" I shot back, grinding my teeth. Something told me this wasn't going to end well.

"I developed you. I trained you. And I have made sure you are all protected. That's how you can trust me." Her eyebrows creased together as we glared at one another.

"Let me talk to the rest of the team and then we will give you our answer." I turned toward Samuel, Audrina and Gave.

"Captain Esa James, you are the leader. Why are you asking their opinion? You make the decision. Now." She stood in the middle of the hallway, her eyes darkening and a knowing smile curving her face. She was taunting me.

I tilted my head as I continued to hold her gaze. "Fine. Go ahead and run your tests."

She nodded. "Good choice. Follow me." She whirled around and marched down the hallway.

I got in line behind her, trying my hardest not to look back at the rest of the team. I already knew what they were thinking; Audrina was very loudly showing me her distrust in her thoughts. She had pulled a small knife from her suit and slowly slid it into her sleeve.

It didn't take long for us to reach Dr. James' lab. The lights were dim inside the small room. On the far wall were several upright glass cylinders.

"What are those?" I asked.

"That's what you will all be getting into so I can do a scan," she said, leaning over a computer.

"What will happen once we are inside?"

"Several lights will come on and then it will be over," she responded, pressing buttons on the screen.

A man with a thick neck and large shoulders walked in. He cleared his throat. "Dr. James, the cryopods are ready for the team."

"Good. Thank you, Reg," she responded, never taking her eyes off the glowing screen in front of her.

The man named Reg began to open the doors to the narrow cylinders and looked back at us. "Please get inside so we can begin."

Samuel walked in front. "I'll go first."

"No. All of you will get into individual cryopods and we will do the testing all at once." Dr. James looked up from her monitor. "Get in."

I didn't want to move; something told me that I should run the other way, but I knew there was no escape. She had us now. I reached for my medallion. We could jump back in time.

"Esa, your medallion doesn't work down here. I've already taken care of that," Dr. James said.

Her words made it seem like we'd never had a relationship, as if she had forgotten she was the reason Samuel and I were even born. Both of my parents seemed so distant, so evil. Had they always been like this? This was one of the many times that I wished I had my memory back.

Samuel and Gave walked ahead of Audrina and me as we all headed toward individual cryopods. I climbed in and looked over at the others. A soft hissing filled the air as the doors sealed. I reached out and pushed at the glass. It wouldn't budge; we were locked inside these contraptions. I tried not to let panic take over. I had to be strong for the team. Dr. James was watching us. More importantly, she was watching me.

I looked at the others and mouthed, "Sorry."

White smoke slowly crept up from the floor of the pod and filled the clear tube.

I glanced around again. Audrina's head had fallen forward. Samuel's did likewise. I could feel my own eyelids grow heavy. Something in the smoke was putting us to sleep. Dr. James had tricked us.

Chapter Fifteen

- -

Chapter Fifteen

My head ached. It felt like a hundred small people were dancing on top of my skull, each of their steps digging deeper and deeper.

"Make it stop," I mumbled. "Make it stop."

No one answered.

The dancing continued, causing more and more pressure.

"Gah!" I yelled, somehow managing to lift my hand to my head. It felt normal.

Suddenly, memories from the cryopods came back to me. Dr. James had given us something to knock us out. My eyes shot open. I had every intention of finding Dr. James and making her pay for what she did to us.

As I struggled to focus, I could tell someone else was in the room with me.

"Hello?" I whispered. "Who's there?"

"Esa, it's me," a male voice responded. "It's Samuel."

The figure walked toward me and slowly came into focus. I stared into his eyes for what seemed like an eternity. "What did she do to us?"

"I don't know. I woke up a little bit ago. I had several minutes to collect my thoughts before I saw your body move."

"Where are the others?"

Samuel stayed silent and pointed to a dark area behind me. I turned to see if Audrina and Gave were there. It was dark, but I could tell there were more tables with bodies lying atop them.

"Do you think she knows we're awake?" I asked, looking at Samuel.

"I don't know. I'm not sure what she knows."

From behind me, I heard someone coughing. Even in the dim light, I could make out the familiar outline of Audrina's body.

"Audrina!" I whispered loudly.

Audrina let out several more quick coughs. "Esa, where are you?"

"Look to your left."

She turned in my direction. "Your mom is an evil witch! I hate her."

"I know. I agree," I responded, silently wondering what she had done. Had Dr. James drugged us for her scientific research, or was I completely wrong?

"What did she do to us?" Audrina asked, her eyes still closed.

"We don't know."

"Okay," Audrina responded in a voice only slightly louder than a whisper as she turned her head the other way.

"Audrina, try to wake up a little more. We probably need to get out of here."

"I know," she mumbled back. "I'm trying." Her eyes remained closed.

A figure on the other side of Audrina suddenly began to cough.

"Gave! Wake up!" Samuel said from somewhere else in the room.

"I'm trying. Give me a few minutes," he responded.

"We don't have time," Samuel said. "Focus. You've got to focus so we can get out of here."

"I'm trying. I'm trying," Gave mumbled back. "My eyelids feel so heavy. I'm not sure I can wake up."

"You can do it," I whispered loudly.

A series of lights flickered on. The room went from dark to light in the matter of seconds.

"You all need to wake up," a deep female voice boomed from somewhere in the darkness.

I looked over at Samuel. He returned my gaze and rolled his eyes. It was our mother talking to us.

Samuel reached up to his neck. "Dr. James, thank you for having us here. We're leaving. Now."

The Jump Line appeared in front of us, and in the next moment, we were back in our house just before it was destroyed. It was a welcome sight.

"What just happened?" I asked.

"She did something to us," Gave said. "Don't you get it? She did something to us!" His voice said it all: he was upset, angry, terrified.

"I get it. Trust me, we all get it," I said through clenched teeth. "We need to calm down and focus."

"How were we able to make the jump?" Audrina asked. "I thought she said our medallions didn't work down there."

"She did say that, but I had a feeling she was lying," Samuel said.

"Somehow I'm not surprised," Gave said.

Samuel cleared his throat. "I jumped to this time because my lab is still intact. Let's go. I need to look at all of you to see exactly what happened to us while we were asleep."

I held out my hand, palm up. It was still empty. "Do you think she has altered our genetic make-up?"

Samuel's extended his hand. He was quiet as he slowly opened his clenched fist. A tiny line of electricity was clearly visible in his palm.

"Why do you still have electricity?" I asked.

"I don't know." Samuel shook his head.

"I want you to check me first," I said, looking deep into his eyes. "Something is different about me and I want answers."

I had felt it even before Dr. James had drugged us. My body was different and it was changing rapidly. I didn't have any electricity running through my veins, but my other senses seemed ultra-heightened. I could see things I hadn't seen before. I could hear conversations that were taking place on the other side of a room. Most importantly, I could easily read anyone's mind.

"I agree," Audrina said. "You can scan me after Esa. I want to know what's going on."

Samuel looked at us. "We still need to find Theo."

At the sound of his name, my stomach sunk to the floor. Theo hadn't made the jump with us. He was still with Dr. James. Sadness took over my thoughts. "Samuel, please go find Theo. I just need to know that he's okay."

"Esa, Theo can handle himself. You need to focus on the rest of the team. What do we do next?" Samuel asked.

He was asking me for some sort of answer...a command. Direction for the entire team. I could hear Dr. James' voice echo in my head. You are a soldier. A leader. I could hear her say, I had no choice, I had to answer.

"Fine. Go ahead and scan us. I will allow you to do some research and then we will go on a search mission for Theo."

"Okay," Samuel said, patting one of the tables. "Hop up here. You will be the first. I'll check the others in a few minutes."

Gave asked, "What do you think she did to us while we were under?"

"I honestly don't know, but I can definitely tell you that I feel different."

"Me too," Gave said. "Me too, and I don't like it. I'm ready to go back and face her again."

"I agree," Samuel responded.

"We need some Intel on that place," Gave said. "Samuel, let me go. I'll jump back in a little bit."

"No," Samuel said in a serious voice. "I want to scan you first."

"Dude, I can be back before you are even done with Esa, I mean, Captain James," he nodded his head in my direction.

I glared back at him. "Gave, we need to stay together right now. I'm not sure we could find you if we got separated."

A look of defeat crossed Gave's face. "Fine," he mumbled. "I'm just getting a little stir crazy. I want to find Theo, and I want to figure out who's been lying to us."

"We all want answers. Trust me, you're not alone."

Chapter Sixteen

C hapter Sixteen

Samuel placed several small objects over my body. Each hovered above me. "Hold still, Esa. This will take a few seconds," he said, looking back at his computer screen.

As the tiny objects floated over me, a hologram of my body appeared next to the bed. The team stood off to the side, studying the image.

"What are these things?" I motioned toward the small devices.

"They're called Oxspys. They allow me to quickly pull all your vital signs, as well as check bone density, and see if any foreign objects have been placed inside you."

"Are they going to touch me or just float above me?"

"They may touch you now and then, but you shouldn't really feel anything. Just stay still. Okay?"

"Fine." I flinched as the tiny objects approached my eyes. Each had a row of lights that hit my skin.

Samuel crossed to another table. "Come on up here, Audrina. I can scan both of you at the same time."

"Works for me," Audrina said, walking over and lying down. Samuel placed several Oxspys above her head.

"Very good. Both of you just lie there while I check my computer and get the information I need."

"Okay," we responded in unison.

Normally, that would have made me laugh, but the mood in the room was too serious. We knew what we needed to do and we knew there wasn't much time. Our bodies were changing and the clock was ticking on finding a way to get off the planet.

Samuel abruptly stopped typing and looked over at Gave. Gave nodded and stepped closer to our tables. Every muscle in his body had tightened.

"What's going on? Both of you have odd looks on your faces." I tried not to move too much as I spoke, but something was definitely up between them.

Neither of the boys responded, but Samuel came over to my table and put his hand on my shoulder. I felt a soft volt of electricity on my skin. "Shh, Esa," he said, holding a finger to his lips as he scanned the room.

"What's happening?" I demanded, lifting my head to look around. Suddenly, I knew. I couldn't feel its presence, but the Hunter was definitely here. It had found us.

"Where is it?" I whispered as panic overtook me.

Samuel didn't respond. Instead, he reached into the space off to his right. I saw the electricity that came out of his hand make contact with something. It formed the thin outline of a body. It definitely looked like it could be

Luther; whoever it was had a stocky build. The figure stumbled back and then disappeared.

We all waited for its next move.

"He's still here," Samuel said through deep breaths. "I can feel him." Samuel took several steps forward and then leaped back as if dodging something.

"Luther! We know it's you," Gave said, posturing for a fight, both his arms up in front of him. "It would be better for all of us if you would just give yourself up."

No sound.

"Luther, we're going to find you and then kill you," Gave continued as he scanned the room.

Just as Gave was finishing his sentence, Audrina let out a guttural sound. "Help me!"

I bounded off the table. Audrina hadn't moved, but tears rolled down her cheeks.

"Audrina, what do you feel?" I screamed.

"It's squeezing me." Her arms began to flail, and she kicked up one of her legs. It came into contact with something.

I threw myself into the air over Audrina, hitting the Hunter hard. The blow caused me to land heavily, but I could tell I had done some damage. There was no way that hadn't hurt him.

Samuel raced over and extended his arm. Nothing this time.

Audrina coughed as she tried to catch her breath. Her tear-streaked cheeks burned with rage. "Samuel, find him. I want that thing to pay for what it just did to me." She got up off of the table, readying herself to fight.

"Esa and I can't feel him," Audrina said to the other two. "You guys need to tell us where he's at."

Gave suddenly spun, pulling two knives from his suit. He sent a bolt of electricity into the metal then threw the knives into the space near Samuel's computer. One of them must have hit its mark because the Hunter made a strange sound. The electrified knife looked like it was floating in the air, but it had obviously pierced Luther's flesh.

"Ha! You're mine now," Gave said, dashing toward Luther's position. But then he glanced back at us. "Samuel, do you feel it?"

"What?" I asked.

"Luther is gone. I can't sense his energy any longer," Gave said.

"Do you think you hurt him?" I asked, staring at the space where Gave had thrown his knives. One still lay on the ground, but the other was gone.

"I hope so," Gave said. Gave was the smallest of our group but had always proven lethal with his knife skills.

"All right. We've been compromised. Let's complete these scans and get out of here before we have any more company. I don't want this thing to attack our secondary or tertiary selves. They won't know what has happened. The fact that he attacked us now means that he was in Dr. James' lab and followed us back here."

"That's a good possibility," Gave said. "I'll be honest, I wasn't really thinking of much when we were back there, so I could easily have missed feeling his energy. I would have just assumed that it was Audrina and Esa, until they mentioned they didn't have their electricity."

Just as I was lying back down on the table, I caught a glimpse of Theo in the hallway outside Samuel's lab. "Theo!" I yelled. "You're here!" I almost ran out of the room, elated at the sight of him.

He glanced over at me and waved, but he didn't enter the room.

Samuel cleared his throat. "Esa, that's not Theo's primary. Remember, we jumped backward. We may see a few more of our other selves if we stay too long, and that always causes problems, because we will instinctively try to ask questions."

"Can the Hunter, I mean Luther, hurt our secondaries or tertiaries?" I asked. "Are they vulnerable right now?"

Our secondaries and tertiaries were older versions of our primaries. It was possible for us to come into contact with younger or older versions of ourselves as we jumped through time, but we had hard rules not to talk to one another. We knew we all existed, but we couldn't warn them of what might happen. It was too risky.

"Fine. Let's finish this," I said, still shaken from the sight of Theo. Hopefully, we would get to see the real Theo soon. Why was Dr. James keeping him, and how had she managed to let us escape?

"Hmm," Samuel mumbled.

"What is it?"

"Your bodies are definitely changing. What do you feel right now?"

"Samuel, I can see your computer screen. I see my body. There's definitely a lot of red inside."

"Yes, I'm not sure what that red is just yet. I'm waiting for the chemical breakdown."

"Esa, jump off. Gave, you go ahead and get up there. I want to compare your body with the girls'."

"Well, first off, my body is going to be much more fly then the girls'," he said nonchalantly as he climbed onto the table. "Don't be a hater, ladies. I just can't help myself. Besides, we all know that I am all lean muscle."

I rolled my eyes.

Samuel also let out a soft chuckle. "Don't worry; I have a feeling the girls would definitely not argue with you."

"That's because there is no argument," Gave shot back as he lay flat on his back.

Audrina pushed Gave's head down. "Oh please. Just lie there and shut up."

"Samuel, control your girlfriend. She's touching me," Gave said raising his head again.

"Gave, you're lucky I no longer have electricity, because I would definitely send a very strong voltage through you right now," Audrina said, crossing her arms.

"You mean like this?" Gave reached out and zapped her. Normally, the movement would have caused a slight jolt, but this time Audrina began to turn blue.

"Audrina, what's happening?" Samuel eyes widened.

"I don't know. I don't feel anything, but my hands are almost glowing."

Gave quickly pulled his hand back, and immediately, the blue disappeared.

We stared at one another silently, wondering what had happened.

"Are you sure you didn't feel anything different?" Samuel asked, his eyes narrowing.

"Promise. I didn't feel anything at all. I didn't even feel Gave touch me. I wouldn't have known anything was off except for your contorted expressions."

Samuel grew serious. "Gave, lie back down. Let's scan you. I need to have something to compare Audrina and Esa's results to, so I can figure out what's going on."

Chapter Seventeen

Chapter Seventeen

Several months ago I'd been a student walking through the hallways of a high school in the year 2010. The old hallways had always smelled of teenage sweat and mildew. There'd been students of all sizes, skin colors and religions at the school, but despite the diversity, I'd always known that I was different.

I had looked different and I definitely hadn't acted like the other students. They'd tried not to make eye contact with me. They must have feared, if I looked them in the eye they would turned to stone, or something along those lines. As if my name was Medusa, instead of Esa.

It had been a lonely time during those three years when I lived in a place called San Diego. The city had always been bustling with activity, but no one had seemed to care about me. Then Samuel had appeared at the high school and everything changed. There'd been something familiar about him. The way he'd looked at me had sent chills through my body.

For some reason, after I had been gone for three years with no memory of who I was, Dr. James had sent Samuel to retrieve me. Why? What had changed to make her want me to return to the year 2105? She was the one who had put me into hiding, and she was the one who took me out. There had to be more to the story. There had to be a reason why. It wasn't Paul, Troy or anyone on the team. It was Dr. Marie James. She was the mastermind behind everything.

I looked over at Samuel, who was placing the Oxspys over Gave. "Did Mom, I mean, Dr. James, ever tell you why she suddenly decided it was time for you to get me?"

"No," he responded, his shoulders slouched. I had no doubt Samuel had wondered the same thing. He was too smart not to put the pieces together. He softly continued, "She just provided me with details on how to find you."

"Anything else? I don't understand what she's up to." I couldn't help the tone of my voice. I knew it sounded accusatory, as if Samuel had been part of the master plan. Maybe he had. Maybe not. One thing I did know: I had been too trusting since my return.

"Maybe she's not up to anything." Samuel shot an icy glare at me. "Esa, not everyone is after us."

His response caused me to take a step back. "Samuel, what aren't you telling me? I'm tired of secrets."

"So am I," he snapped. "You and Dr. James were working on something when you disappeared. Esa, you volunteered to go."

"That's what we've been told, but who really knows the truth?" My hands shot up into the air as I vented my frustration. Dr. James, Paul, Troy and Luther all had their own agendas. Did they care about any of us on the team or were we just their little science experiments.

"All I know is, you and Dr. James were plotting something, and then you were gone. Think about it, Esa. You're not really a victim but more of an accomplice."

His words cut me to the core. This was a different side of Samuel. He was angry.

"I'm sorry," I finally managed to whisper. "I didn't realize how you felt."

He straightened and put his hands on his hips. "Let me tell you how I felt. I felt abandoned. None of my family trusted me enough to fill me in on a plan that they had apparently been working on for a while."

"I didn't mean to hurt you," I said softly placing my hand on his shoulder. "You have to believe me, Samuel. I don't remember what happened, but I know I would never intentionally hurt you."

"Esa, for a while, I considered you dead. You understand that, right? You were dead to me." His jaw muscles tightened and he looked back down at Gave.

"I'm sorry," I mumbled again, but I couldn't help but think about his words. There was something in the way he was talking that scared me, but it also made me realize how screwed up everything was.

Beep. Beep. Beep.

The tiny Oxspys moved over Gave's body, stopping at various points, making odd noises.

After several seconds, Samuel turned to his screen. "Hmm. Just as I thought."

"What?" Audrina asked, peering over his shoulder.

"It's different. Completely different," Samuel said, pointing to the outline of Gave's body. "Your bodies are changing, but ours are the same."

Samuel studied us, as if he waiting for an answer.

"Something must have happened after the shooting," I responded, looking over at Audrina. "Maybe it was Paul who did something to us."

"Jerk." Audrina sneered. She clenched her fists and punched the top of the metal table. "I swear, both of your parents are crazy."

"What does that mean?" I had to agree with her that both Dr. and General James seemed self-centered and odd, but I really didn't want someone else to judge my parents.

"It means they don't care about us, Esa! Don't you get it? They have set us up time and time again. I'm scared that one day I won't have anyone on this team by my side. It's absolutely horrible." Audrina's bottom lip began to quiver as she wrapped her arms protectively around herself.

"Don't worry, Audrina. I'm not going to let anything happen to the team," Samuel said, placing an arm over her shoulders.

I looked my teammate square in the eyes. "Neither am I." She had to know that she could trust me. This team was everything to me. They were my friends...my family.

Samuel glanced at another monitor. "Crap. It's time for us to go," he said, grabbing ahold of his medallion. We all jumped without looking back, knowing someone was just outside the door.

Chapter Eighteen

C hapter Eighteen

We landed in Samuel and Audrina's place in the middle of snowy nowhere. The cold air smacked me hard in the face as the Jump Line closed.

"Why did we come back here?" I looked at Samuel, frustrated to once again see this frozen place. It was honestly the last place I wanted to be right now, since it was so close to Dr. James.

"It's the only place we have in our primary year that is safe. Where else did you want to go?" Audrina asked. "Besides, this place has the technology and tools we need if we are going to put together any sort of plan."

"I get it—we have this place and its safe—but Dr. James knows we're here. I bet she's tracking us right now."

Samuel chuckled. "Oh please, Esa, she's been tracking us since day one. Nothing has changed, except now we know she's alive and watching our every move."

I took a deep breath as his words sunk in. It was true. The one thing that had changed was our knowledge about her. She was alive, and apparently very much aware of our situation.

Gave finally interjected, "Besides, this site places us closer to Theo."

"Theo," I repeated, trying to think clearly. We definitely needed to get Theo back. He was one of our strongest soldiers and would know what to do next.

Samuel tilted his chin. "Esa, did Theo fall into the water or did it seem like something grabbed him and pulled him in?"

"I don't know." I thought back to the moment everything had happened. "Theo slipped on some ice, but it seemed like something he could recover from. Instead, he kept falling until he hit the water."

"Think about his facial expression. Do you think he knew what was happening? After all, he is the one who wanted to go exploring," Samuel said, rubbing his chin. His eyes had glossed over, as if he were thinking back to the last time he had seen Theo.

I didn't like where Samuel was going with this line of questioning. There was no way Theo had willingly gone into that water. "He definitely seemed surprised when he slipped. He tried to grab onto something, but it seemed like his arms weren't long enough. It was almost as if something was blocking him from taking my hand."

Audrina looked over at Samuel and nodded. "I just saw Esa's thoughts. She's telling the truth, Samuel. Theo looked surprised and tried to grab for something, but he couldn't seem to connect with anything."

Samuel looked at both of us. "Can you really read each other's minds? That seems unreal."

"Yes!" we both blurted out. Our joint response made us giggle. It felt good to have some laughter to cut through the tension.

"I don't understand what happened, but suddenly I know what Audrina is thinking and, apparently, vice versa."

"That's right," Audrina said with a wicked smile. "I know all of Esa's deep dark secrets."

"You don't know all of my secrets," I quickly responded. It would be impossible for her to know everything when I couldn't even remember what my life had been like before three years ago.

Samuel glanced at Gave and then finally spoke. "This might actually be a good thing. Esa, try to think back to the car accident when you first landed in the year 2007. Maybe Audrina can watch and see if she spots anything from your viewpoint. We saw it from our viewpoints, but we know there's something there we've missed."

"It's definitely worth a try," I responded, not really sure what Audrina might be able to see. I had thought back to the day of the accident many times. It seemed like it had just happened yesterday, even though it was three years ago.

The familiar sound of metal scrapping against metal filled my head. My thoughts were back at the accident scene. There was the burning smell that filled the air and suddenly a bright light. I was walking around in a daze. It felt like my eyes were having a hard time adjusting. There was smoke everywhere. Two cars were in front of me. Their mangled metal exteriors were wrapped oddly around each other. There were no other sounds, only the smell of something burning. I hadn't noticed it before, but I felt something on my lower back, like a hand. It pushed me forward slightly, as if to stop me from walking away from the accident scene.

I shook my head, trying to clear my thoughts. "I felt something, but I'm not sure what."

"I could tell," Audrina whispered. "Esa, you definitely weren't alone at that crash site." Audrina sounded so sure of herself that it made me uneasy, but also very curious...and mad.

"Who was there?" I asked. I wanted to know so badly.

Audrina closed her eyes. "I don't know. I didn't see anything either, but I definitely felt the presence of someone in the area. It was odd, but whoever it was, they touched you."

"Do you think it was Luther?" I asked; although, it seemed impossible. Luther had only recently become invisible, but maybe he had been able to do this all along.

"It's possible," Audrina responded without hesitation as she thought about Luther. I could clearly see his face in her thoughts. "I guess anything is possible."

"What about that flash of light?" I asked. "Did you see anything?"

Audrina was still lost in thought. I saw the accident play over and over in her mind. After several seconds, she let out a snort. "Oh, I can tell you who was there, and what that bright flash was all about."

"What?" I almost yelled, eager to know more about what had happened on that day. "Tell me. Please."

"It was the prestigious Dr. James. I saw her look at you, and then the bright light was her disappearing."

I raised my hands to cover my ears. "The bright light," I echoed. "The bright light."

There was something about that light. That wasn't the only time I'd seen it.

My hand flew to my mouth. "Oh my God. The light. That's the key. She doesn't travel on the Jump Line. She's created a new mode of transportation, and it includes a very white, bright light."

The room grew quiet. No one said anything in response until, finally, Audrina looked up. "I saw the bright light during the shooting in the hallway. Esa and I dropped to the ground. The light was all around us."

"What happened next for you?" I pressed.

She stared straight ahead, but there was only darkness in her thoughts.

In my mind, I saw images of the beautiful white tiger stalking toward me.

Audrina met my gaze. "I didn't see a tiger. It was dark, and then I woke in Paul's lab."

She bit down on her lower lip as she thought about the lab. I could see everything so clearly. Audrina was remembering the dimly lit laboratory that all of them had been in on a few occasions.

Audrina whipped her head around to look at Samuel. "Did you guys not see the bright light? I remember it being so bright that it caused my eyes to water."

Samuel paused for a second and then responded. "I remember seeing a quick flash of light, but before anything else happened, Theo had grabbed his medallion and the Jump Line opened. We were gone before anyone else could follow. I thought the two of you were with us, but I quickly discovered I was wrong."

"Samuel's right," Gave said. "Everything happened so fast. It wasn't until we landed that we realized it was just the three of us. We searched for you both, but we couldn't find you for several weeks."

I shook my head "We're being played. It's time for us to pay a visit to someone we all know. Trust me, that person is waiting for us."

Chapter Nineteen

Chapter Nineteen

Instantly, we were back in OnyxFive, in a large office.

"Why are we here?" Audrina whispered.

"You'll see."

Before I had a chance to say anything else, the door to the room flew open. On the other side stood General Paul James, a smug look on his face.

Audrina's eyes widened. "Crap," she said under her breath. "I knew at some point we would see him again, but I was really hoping to avoid him for at least the next decade or so."

"I knew you'd be back," he said, his eyes narrowing as he studied our faces.

"Of course you did." I stepped to the front of the group. "We paid a visit to Artek. Dr. James was a little surprised."

"I'm sure she was."

Samuel took a step forward. "Aren't you shocked to hear that she's alive?"

Paul let out a sigh. "No. I've known she was alive for quite a while. And she already warned me that you would be stopping by."

Samuel didn't hesitate. In one swift move, he had Paul pinned to the wall.

"What else aren't you telling us? These little games are getting old," Samuel asked through clenched teeth. I had never seen him this mad before. His entire demeanor had changed. He was consumed by rage. "You told me that she was dead, that you had found her body."

"It wasn't my doing. She wanted all of you to believe she was dead. It was the only way she would be safe to continue her work. She also knew someone on the team was working against us, and she needed to get that person—who we all know now is Luther—off her trail," Paul said as a look of pain crossed his face. "She figured out a new way to travel through time and was about to finish her research when Troy paid her a visit. She knew she had to take protective measures, which is how Esa became a part of the plan."

"Is that really what she wanted, or is it what you both wanted?" I asked, shaking at the realization that Samuel and I had been duped by our own parents. They had lied to us both repeatedly because of their obsession with science. Maybe it wasn't even about science, but rather ego.

Paul pushed away from Samuel. "Let me down, Captain Samuel James. That is an order."

Samuel glared at him but finally took a step back. "Fine, but we want answers. Now."

"Okay," he said, smoothing out his shirt. A dark red mark was left on his neck, with the outline of Samuel's hand.

"Your mother and I knew there was a mole. We suspected Luther, but we also questioned whether or not Theo might be connected," Paul said.

"Wait. Why did you think Theo was a traitor, and why are you only telling us this now?" I asked. There was no way Theo could be a traitor. He was the leader.

"We tracked him to NorthStar," Paul said, his eyebrows arching. "There were other things as well. Esa, we approached you about the possibility. You were angry at first, but then you also started tracking Theo. You, too, found him at NorthStar."

Images of NorthStar came rushing back into my thoughts. When we had been there, everything had seemed so familiar. I knew I'd been inside before, but I hadn't remember being there because of Theo.

"You became very upset. We all worried that our secrets were getting into the wrong hands, so your mother hid the information and then, as a precautionary measure, she put a clue on you, in case something happened to us. You were jumping to 2007 to give us the insurance we needed that Luther wouldn't go against us. This time, you weren't jumping to pull a body but to kill someone—Luther's grandfather. But something happened during the jump and you lost your memory. We think you hit something during transit. Dr. James saw what happened. She thought about pulling you back, but then we realized this might be the perfect plan. If you were hidden, we at least had some hope that if someone tried to mess with our team, we had you safely hidden away. So, she went back and put something inside your body that would prevent the rest of the team from feeling your energy. It was remarkable science. I have to admit, I was impressed with her work that day."

Rage ignited inside of me. I wasn't entirely sure I believed Paul's story. Why was he only divulging this information now? We had talked back at NorthStar. He had told me a modified version of the story then, but the added parts made a big difference.

"You left me there for three years." I seethed. Three years was a long time, too long of a time for someone to leave their child.

"Yes, because we were trying to collect more evidence. We weren't ready for you to come back. Plus, the war continued to wage on. We weren't entirely sure we would survive," Paul said. "It was safer for us to know that at least one of you was hidden with information that could hopefully save your mother's work."

"Three years!" I yelled again. "It shouldn't have taken you three years to figure out the truth. In the meantime, you destroyed my life."

Paul shook his head. "Don't forget, I also couldn't get on the line. Your mom thought it would be a giveaway that we were working together, and she wanted Troy and everyone to believe that she had died, so she would be able to work on quietly, including getting into Troy's lab, if need be. I had no way to visit you, Esa."

Samuel looked over at him. "So, you finally convinced me to take you on the line?"

"Yes. I was tired of all of you being able to travel through time while I was stuck in this year. We know the world is dying. I don't intend to be here when it does." Paul looked over at me. "Esa, it was a mission, and one you volunteered for at the time. You knew the length of the mission was not set."

"No. I was protecting all of you. But who was protecting me when you sent me off alone?" I said as a single tear slid down my warm cheek.

Paul shook his head, a look of disgust on his face. "You're a soldier. Stop crying."

My back went rigid at his statement.

Audrina moved forward. "So, what grand plan do you and Dr. James have up your sleeves?"

A gleam flickered in Paul's eyes. "We're not limited. It's time we unlock all of our capabilities."

"What do you mean?" I asked, folding my arms over my chest.

"I mean that this team has the right capabilities to be able to go to another planet, another solar system, and start over. We've developed a new way to travel, and I think we can now do it," Paul said. "It's time for us to go and visit Dr. James at Artek."

Chapter Twenty

C hapter Twenty

A big part of me didn't want to look into her eyes again. She was the person who had caused so much hurt and pain. It seemed as if she didn't even have a soul. There was nothing warm about her.

"Why do we need to go back to Artek now? Are you sure she even wants to see us?" I asked, trying to make sense of my internal emotional struggle. She scared me, but she also intrigued me. We were probably more alike than I wanted to admit.

"I've already talked to her. It's time for you all to hear the truth before we take the next step," Paul said, cutting into my thoughts.

"What is the next step?" Samuel asked. I could tell he, too, was trying to process everything. If we went back to Artek, would we be in danger?

"You'll see. I'm not prepared to show you." Paul's eyes suddenly darkened again. The look caused me to take a step backward.

"Wait!" I put my hands on my hips. "What aren't you telling us?"

Paul smirked. "There's a lot I haven't told you, but, quite honestly, I don't think you're prepared to hear the entire story."

"Try us," Audrina said, raising her eyebrows. "We might surprise you."

"I don't know if you are mature enough to hear the entire story," Paul responded.

The response caused Audrina's face to go from ivory to crimson in two seconds flat.

"Paul, I don't need to be here. Let's get that straight. I'm tired of all these games you and Dr. James are putting us through, and I'm definitely tired of you altering my genetic make-up without my consent. The last time I checked, this is my body." Audrina crossed her arms over her chest.

"No. You're wrong," Paul said, a evil smile pulling at the corners of his mouth. "All of you signed agreements when you first joined, giving us full authority over your bodies. You're not in control; I am."

"We'll see about that," I mumbled, hating Paul more than ever. He had no right to speak to any of us in this awful tone.

"Let me get one thing very clear, Esa. You are biologically my daughter, but, more importantly, you are also a soldier designed and trained by OnyxFive. Your allegiance is to us and no one else."

"No. You've got that very wrong. My allegiance is to this team," I responded, clenching my fists. I wasn't going to let Paul get away with telling me whom I needed to obey. The one thing I was sure about in this world was that this team was my family, not Paul, and definitely not Dr. James. Especially after everything I had heard and seen over the past few hours.

Paul began to laugh. "You can't run from me this time. I will find you."

"Who said we were going to run?" Gave asked. "We don't run, we jump."

Samuel lunged for Paul and sent a volt of electricity through his body, causing him to fall backward, twitching, against the wall.

Gave tugged at his medallion. "Let's go!"

We all leaped onto the Jump Line before Paul could recover from the attack. I glanced back for a brief second and saw Paul staring at me as we disappeared. I knew he would find us. There was no way he was going to let us get away. He was right: he would definitely be tracking us.

"Where are we going?" I couldn't help but ask.

"We're going to 2010, Esa. It's a year you're most familiar with," Samuel said.

"Ugh. I don't want to go back to 2010."

But before I could say anything else, we landed in a heavily wooded area. Large trees with lush green leaves loomed high above us. The sky was grey, and then I remembered...it had rained the last time I was in 2010. We tended to jump back in time to places and times that were familiar to us. This was the day when Samuel found me.

"Why are we here again?" Gave whispered as we all looked around, trying to get our bearings.

"I think this is probably a pretty safe year. Because we've all jumped to this year so many times, our current energy might be masked by our secondaries and tertiaries. We just need to stay out of sight of any normals," Samuel said, crouching behind a large tree as he surveyed the area.

"Or we could just find some real clothes and cover these outfits so we blend in with the rest of society," I responded, pinching at the white fabric.

"How are we going to find clothes when we're in the middle of nowhere?" Audrina asked.

"Let's hide out here until nightfall. Then we can jump into a store in town and acquire some clothes," Samuel said.

It wasn't a bad idea. The lush landscape would definitely provide us with some cover.

"We also need some sort of shelter," I whispered. "We need somewhere we can go to while we get back on our feet, so we can rescue Theo."

Samuel looked over at me. "I have a better plan. I thought 2010 was the year we should land in, but I really think we should be in 2105." His eyes lit up. "We need to go to NorthStar. We need to figure out what's really going on."

We all stood there silently as we took in what Samuel was saying. 2105. NorthStar. It was a risky move. The last time we were there, we had blown up most of the facility.

"What's the latest on Luther and Troy? Do we know where they're at?" Audrina asked. "We probably need some Intel on them before we go back to their turf."

"No." Samuel shook his head. "I think Luther has just been leading us on a wild goose chase to keep us busy and away from Troy while they finish getting things ready for their next mission to Merak. Our last visit to NorthStar probably accelerated their timetable."

"I'd love to pay that slime bag another visit," Audrina said, pulling at a lock of her long white hair. "It's been a little too long since I've seen his ugly face."

Samuel stared at her for several seconds. "We're not paying anyone a visit. The goal is to stay out of sight while we figure out what's going on. We may need to separate, to keep our energy levels down, but the key is to observe and see if we can figure out the truth."

"No, we won't have to do that," I responded.. "Remember, Audrina and I no longer have electricity. Can you feel any energy coming from us?"

Samuel and Gave both shook their heads. "No." "Good point."

"At least it will make us harder to find," Audrina said, but we both knew that it was scary to no longer have electricity coursing through our veins. It had been one of our most powerful weapons.

"Why did Paul alter us?"

"It obviously wasn't Paul," Gave said. "It was Dr. James. My guess is, she grabbed both of you and took you to Artek for the majority of the time and then, right as you were both about to wake, she moved you to OnyxFive."

"Maybe." I wondering who else might be a part of this game. The sound of someone running toward us caused my head to jerk around. "We need to get out of here. Someone is coming," I said, grabbing my medallion before we came face-to-face with whoever was out in the woods.

Chapter Twenty-One

Chapter Twenty-One

We landed near a metallic dumpster in an alleyway. It was the same alley we'd been in not long ago. I glanced at my watch to see if we were in the primary state or if we'd travelled back in time slightly. I knew we were in the year 2105, but without my watch, I wouldn't know exactly what day of the year. My watch let me know we were in our primary time. It was the 96th day of the year 2105.

NorthStar was right around the corner. Or at least the remnants of North-Star were around the corner.

This was the first time I had jumped back to this place and time. I still hadn't seen the destruction we had left behind when we set off several explosive devices inside the large research facility, but I remembered clearly the deafening sound of the building crumbling to the ground. We had done the right thing destroying the facility. Troy and Luther were being reckless going back in time and taking healthy humans. At some point it would have caught up with us, causing too many ripples in time.

The air was thick, and a lingering burning smell made it feel like a piece of sandpaper had magically appeared in the back of my throat, scratching my skin. My eyes began to water. Instantly, we all coughed from the dust.

Gave covered his mouth as he leaned over, trying to control his coughing. He remained hunched as we tried to acclimate.

Samuel put his finger to his lips. "Stay here," he whispered as he crept forward, pausing every few steps to listen. When he finally made it to the corner, he leaned against the brickwork and carefully peered around the building's sharp corner.

His lanky body looked like a snake as it wrapped around the edge. He stayed there for what seemed like an eternity, while we all hung back in the middle of the alley, looking around at the other buildings to see if we had been spotted.

A creepy feeling settled in around us. It felt as if someone was watching our every move, or maybe it was just my imagination because I knew we were close to an enemy. Too close. Luther and Troy were somewhere around here. I had no doubt that they had come back to salvage NorthStar. Troy had too much invested into the facility to let it disappear.

The only sound at the moment was that of helicopter rotors, off in the distance. With each passing second, the sound grew more and more faint.

Gave let out another little cough, and I turned to him to put my finger to my lips, just as Samuel had done a few seconds ago. Gave looked back at me with pleading eyes. He was trying to get control of his cough, but couldn't seem to find a pocket of clean air.

"Samuel!" Audrina whispered loudly, trying to get his attention. "Samuel!"

Samuel's shot around as he looked back at us, and then he reluctantly waved us over. Again he put his finger to his lips. Audrina rolled her eyes this time.

Great, I thought as I followed behind her. This was just what we all needed right now: Audrina and Samuel to be at odds about something. It wasn't the first time things had been tense between them; it was becoming part of my new normal. They loved each other, but they also got on each other's nerves...a lot.

"I thought I asked you all to be quiet," Samuel said as we got closer, his eyes never leaving Audrina's.

Audrina shot an icy glare back at him. "We were quiet, while you took all the time in the world to check out the scenery."

Samuel stared back at Audrina before finally responding in a hesitant voice. "Okay. Sorry."

Audrina put her hands on her hips and rocked back and forth, as if trying to calm herself down before saying anything else.

Samuel nodded at her and then turned back in the direction of the main roadway. "You guys will want to see this."

We peered around the corner, unsure what scene would greet us. North-Star had once been a very large building, with many stories above ground and many more below. It had been massive, with few windows and even fewer opportunities for anyone to escape.

Right before we had set the chargers, we had seen a number of people inside, but Paul had said we didn't have a choice, we had to destroy the compound. Destroying the building meant we had to kill or severely injure everyone inside, except for the normals in the holding room.

Now, before us stood a crumbled mess. The once-massive building was nothing more than a pile of debris, with chucks of concrete exterior lying at odd angles.

"Gah." I couldn't help but let out the odd noise. I knew we had placed a number of explosives around the building—enough to destroy it—but actually seeing the remains was surreal. It felt like we were on a movie set. This didn't happen in real life.

The area around the building was empty. My eyes widened as reality set in. Had Paul tricked us into killing so many innocents?

"It's too quiet," I said.

"I know," Samuel responded. "That's what I was thinking. It's eerie."

"Oh my God. What did we do?" Audrina gasped. "We killed them. We killed all of them. I knew we couldn't trust Paul. I knew it."

I looked at Samuel. "We can travel through time, right?"

"Yes."

"Then how did we not see this happening?" I asked; although, I had a feeling he was wondering the same thing.

He shook his head and stared back at me. "We can't travel into the future, but still, we should have traveled to NorthStar more often, to keep an eye on it and what Troy was doing. We had Intel from the normals living in the tunnels. Unfortunately, I think most of it was wrong."

"Samuel, this is on us. We are responsible. We killed more humans." I threw up my hands, growing angrier by the second. I had seen so much devastation since my return to this time two months ago. Sometimes it was overwhelming to see how different things had become in the future. "We did this!"

"I know!" he yelled back at me, running his hand through his chalky-white hair. Finally, in a softer voice, he said again, "I know. We should have done more recon."

"Do you know something you're not telling us?" I demanded.

Samuel's eyes looked tired. "Esa, we're being played."

"What does that mean?" He had to give me more than that.

"This scene doesn't feel right. Nothing feels right anymore. Too many people are being hurt." His shoulders sagged as if the weight of the world had suddenly fallen on them.

"We're going to figure it out." I hoped I was right.

I looked toward the hazy blue sky and wondered where Luther and Troy were hiding. Then I thought back to Theo. He was still at Artek. It was time for us to go and get him. We needed him on this team.

"Esa, I recalled what you said about Paul and Troy. I think they're all working together, but they don't know it. I think Mom might be a bigger part of this problem than we ever thought," Samuel said.

Chapter Twenty-Two

C hapter Twenty-Two

Samuel's eyes suddenly widened. He looked over at Gave, who slowly nodded.

"He's back, isn't he?" I said, knowing the Hunter was here. I couldn't feel its energy, but I knew he was here and close. Too close.

"Where is he?" I stammered, hoping Samuel would point to somewhere far away.

Samuel didn't budge for several seconds. He looked at me and slowly shook his head. After several seconds, he puffed out his chest. "Who are you and what do you want?" he asked the empty space...behind me.

Suddenly, I could sense movement. Whatever, or whoever, it was, they were close to me. I could feel warm breath on the back of my neck. It sent chills down my spine as I braced for its next move.

My breath quickened. I had to get control of this situation; although, I wasn't sure any more about my body's special enhancements or capabilities. So much had changed recently. I honestly didn't know what I could do right now. I hadn't trained since someone had altered my internal components to no longer allow electricity to flow through my veins. I was almost normal.

I wished there had been more time to assess the situation, but time was not my friend right now. Instead, I swung my right arm backward, without hesitation and with all of my might. I wanted it to connect with something. Anything. I also wanted to cause pain.

I felt the Hunter's muscles as my fist came into contact with its skin. It didn't flinch from the blow. I pulled back my hand and tried to ignore the pain that shot through my entire arm. It felt like my fist had come into contact with a brick wall.

Instead of pondering what had happened, I spun to face the empty space behind me. It was hard fighting something you couldn't see, but I knew it was there, and I would let it know my fury.

I lifted my right leg, with the intent of kicking at the space in front of me multiple times, but Samuel grabbed my shoulder. "Esa, it's gone. I don't feel its energy anymore."

"What?" I spun back around to face my brother, trying not to lose my balance. "Why did it leave so quickly?"

Samuel shook his head. "I don't know. I wish I had a better answer, but it's the truth...I don't know. What I do know is that it's gone."

"I wonder why he didn't do anything to any of us this time. What is Luther trying to prove?" Gave said.

"That's a good question. This is all starting to give me a massive headache." Audrina squatted, and rubbed her temples.

We were alone again, but obviously someone knew we were here. I couldn't help but look skyward. I scanned the buildings, seeking any sign that someone was watching us. We were easy targets right now. We were standing in an empty alley without any cover.

"We need to get out of here," I whispered, suddenly scared of what the future might hold. "I don't like it. I don't like it at all."

Gave nodded. "I agree. This place is giving me a bad feeling."

Without hesitation, we all jumped on the line and landed inside our old house. Its plain white walls were a welcome sight after all we had been through. I had visited the house several times, but every time I had come back, I realized I didn't want to leave, and that had put our existence into question. After all, we couldn't change history; not without it affecting the future.

"Yes! I'm so happy to see this place!" Audrina squealed with delight next to me. Her excitement slowly faded, however, as reality set in, and I saw a random tear escape from one of her eyes and slide down her cheek. "I'm sorry. This craziness is starting to get to me. This is the one place that feels safe."

I pulled Audrina into a hug. "I know, and I agree," I whispered into her ear.

We had been through so much recently that any sign of normalcy was welcome. I thought back to what Paul had said about me being a soldier, but I was also human. So was the rest of the team, and he hadn't made it to where we couldn't feel emotions. Maybe it would have been easier if Dr. James had done that to us, made it so we didn't care.

Samuel's voice cut through my thoughts. "We jumped back to a year before we had to destroy the house. I really just need time to think."

"Is there anywhere in this house we could hide and not be spotted?" I asked, hoping the answer would be yes. At least we felt safe in this space. "The basement," Samuel responded, pausing to think about what he had said. Finally, he cleared his throat. "We should be safe down there for a little bit. Let's go."

Samuel walked us down several narrow hallways and then down a back set of stairs. The basement proved as clean as the rest of the house, with stark white walls and several large metal tables.

"What did we use this space for?" I asked, unsure what I was looking at.

"For a very brief period, it was my lab, but then I was able to build a better one upstairs. This space has stayed empty ever since," Samuel responded as he walked around the room. "The only problem we might have is—"

"Good evening, Captain James," said a familiar robotic voice.

"I was about to say, the only problem we might have is LUX," Samuel whispered, before hesitantly turning to the screen mounted on the wall.

"Good evening, LUX. How are you today?"

"I am good. Thank you for asking." The human-like image stared, emotionless.

"We are good as well," Samuel said.

"Captain James, from what year did you travel?" LUX asked as she looked at each one of us questioningly.

"Twenty-one-zero-five, but we've been traveling a lot lately and need some rest. We will have to stay here for a bit. Is there any way you can make sure the primaries for this year don't venture down here? I don't want them to wonder why we would be back visiting and needing a place to sleep," Samuel said.

"I understand and will oblige," LUX responded, before disappearing from the screen.

"Good. That will give us a little time. We can't let the others see us. They will wonder what's going on," Samuel said sternly to the rest of us.

We all nodded in agreement, but I secretly wondered how LUX would make sure no one spotted us.

"Are you sure it's safe?" I asked Samuel in a whisper.

"No, but it's the only place for us to stay while we get things figured out," he responded, draping his arm over my shoulder.

It felt good to have my brother standing so close to me. "Okay. I get it."

Samuel chuckled. "No, you don't. We've got quite the battle ahead of us, but right now, I need you to get some rest so we can be ready to fight...when needed."

"Okay," I said as my eyes grew heavy. I wanted to stay awake, but it was no use. We had jumped too many times over the past few hours and my body was exhausted. I needed rest. I needed food. I needed my family.

"Samuel, what happened to make our family so dysfunctional?" I muttered.

"Shh," he responded. "Our family is not dysfunctional. It's only our parents. We are normal, and willing to fight for the lives of many others. Unfortunately, our parents think differently."

I leaned my head against his shoulder. "What will happen to them?"

He paused for several seconds and then softly rubbed his finger against my cheek. "Esa, we will need to stand up to them. It's the only way for us to survive."

I thought about what he had said. "Okay. I will fight."

Chapter Twenty-Three

Chapter Twenty-Three

I said I would fight, but really I just wanted to survive. The world had become a harsh place in which to live, but I wanted to live. I wanted to breathe the air. I wanted to run through the forests. This was my world, and I wasn't ready to give up.

It was time we figured out our next move, but I couldn't will myself to do it without Theo. He should have been here, guiding me, telling me what to do, but instead he was at Artek. Was he being held against his will? Surely, if he were okay, he would have managed to escape and find us.

I hadn't seen him for what seemed like an eternity, except in my thoughts and dreams. If only there were a way for me to see him right now. To touch him. To know that everything was okay. What had Dr. James done to him? Had she altered him too? The idea made me want to vomit, or hit something with a bolt of electricity. But then I remembered: I no longer had the latter option. I had become like the normals, and it was frustrating and scary.

A wave of loneliness washed over me. It was time to go and get Theo.

Slowly, I slid my legs over the side of the small table on which I had been lying for the past few hours. At least, that's how long I assumed I'd been asleep. Everyone else lay motionless on nearby tables in the middle of the dark basement.

"What are you doing?" Audrina groggily whispered, causing my back to go rigid.

I had assumed they were all hard asleep and hadn't expected the sound of her voice.

"Go back to sleep. I'm just stretching," I responded, hoping she would do as I said and not ask additional questions.

"Okay," she mumbled, before going quiet again.

I tip-toed to the far end of the basement and stood silently against the wall, watching the others.

Was I really ready to face Dr. James alone? In my mind, I knew the answer: yes. I could do it. I was a warrior. A soldier. My mother's daughter.

If only I had done a better job at recon and knew more about Artek. That would be ideal, but, quite honestly, I didn't have the time. I needed to go now, before the others woke and tried to stop me.

I traced the thin silver medallion that gleamed from my chest. Its metal surface easily stood out against my white uniform. I had let my fingers slid over the outline of this necklace so many times over the past few years. The medallion was the one thing I had always had. At least, as far as I could remember.

Without hesitation, I pulled at it. I was going to Artek, and I was going to bring back Theo. I turned briefly to look back at the others. They lay motionless on the tables. I could hear Gave's soft breathing. I would be back before they woke. With that thought, I turned and jumped.

Instantly, I was standing in a large room. I had been here before; it was the room with the white tiger. This time, I knew I wasn't dreaming. I shook my head several times, trying to clear my thoughts. I needed to go on a little hunt of my own.

I darted for the only door in the room, grasped the cold, metal handle, and pulled it open. A stark white hallway greeted me on the other side, and I made my way down the narrow space until I reached another door. Crap. I didn't know if this was the right door. Honestly, I had no clue what I was looking for, other than I knew that Theo was somewhere inside this facility.

The door made a soft clicking sound as the handle released, and it swung open to reveal Theo sitting hunched over behind a glass wall. It was as if he were being held in a cage.

"Theo!" I frantically whispered. "Theo! I found you!" I tried to contain my excitement, but pure emotion gave way to commonsense.

"Esa!" His gaze darted to me as he jumped up from where he was sitting.. "Esa, listen to me; you've got to go back. Tell Samuel I need him. He's the only one who can help me."

"Shut up," I responded angrily. "I'm not leaving without you." I looked him over. His medallion no longer hung around his neck.

His eyes widened. "You have to go now. It's only a matter of seconds before they come in here. Go, Esa. Tell Samuel he needs to come to Artek."

"No."

"Esa, go!" he yelled. "That's an order." I could hear the panic in his voice, but he had to know I was strong. I could handle anyone who walked through the door.

"No! I'm not leaving." I wasn't going to budge.

His expression softened. "Esa, go now. Trust me. Tell Samuel I know who has been hunting the team, but he has to come here. I need to talk with him and only him."

I shook my head. I didn't want to leave Artek without him, but Theo didn't want to see me. He had been hoping Samuel would find him. He didn't think I was capable of getting him out of this situation. I would prove him wrong. I tugged on my medallion again. Instantly, I was standing next to Theo. The glass wall between us was now off to one side.

Theo had a sly smile on his face. "Why did you do that?"

"I'm not leaving without you." I was tired of everyone questioning my abilities.

Theo hesitated for several seconds before saying, "Okay, let's go. I need to talk with the rest of the team."

"About what?" I asked, perplexed. There was something about his voice that didn't seem quite right and made the tiny hairs on the back of my neck stand up.

"Esa! Let's get out of here," he responded harshly. "Isn't that what you wanted me to say?"

My hand shook as I pulled at my medallion, and I decided not to open the Jump Line. Theo didn't seem himself. In a rush of realization, I knew what was happening. This person wasn't my Theo. It was an imposter.

Someone who'd lured me in and tried to get me to bring back the rest of the team...most notably Samuel.

The idea ignited a new wave of anger inside me. I would make this person pay. My fists slowly tightened. Adrenaline coursed through my veins. I leaned in, ready to put as much energy as possible behind the blow that I intended for the imposter's face. I felt the contact as my fist hit his right cheekbone. The impact caused me to take a step backward.

The thing that looked like Theo had a snarl on its face as it tried to process what I had done. Suddenly, it looked sad, "Esa, what are you doing?" it asked, raising its hands to physically inspect the damage I had done.

"Shut up. I know you're not Theo," I spat out as I walked around him.

"Esa, you need to calm down. This is not how you normally act," the fake Theo responded calmly, almost robotically.

"I don't know who you are, but I'm going to destroy you," I said as I lunged forward with of my fist ready to make contact.

Just as I grazed the imposter's skin, I heard the words, "Well done, Captain Esa James. You have passed the test."

What? What test? My gaze shot up toward the ceiling. "Thank you, Dr. James. I've come to take Theo home."

There was a brief pause and then the voice responded with, "Very well. Go back to the hallway and go down two more doors. Theo will be waiting for you."

"And who else will be there?" I asked through deep breaths.

"Only Theo. The real Theo. I am done with him, but I would like Samuel to come and visit me. Please let him know we need to discuss something."

"Fine." I turned toward the half-inch-thick sheet of glass. It slid downward and I strode to the door that led back to the hallway.

Once I entered the narrow space again, I began to count the doors. "One, two." Two! That's what she had said. This was the door that separated me from Theo.

I pushed it open and there he stood, near the back of the room with his hands on his hips.

"Well, it's about time," he said. "What took you so long?"

A wave of emotion overcame me. This was my Theo. He was standing so close to me. I rushed into the room and wrapped my arms around his neck. "I'm so happy to see you," I murmured.

He leaned down. "Me too, but we seriously need to get out of here."

"I know. I know," I responded, trying to get control of my emotions.

"Esa, pull your medallion."

"Why don't you open the Jump Line?"

"Uh, I don't have my medallion any longer," he responded, making odd hand gestures toward his white suit. He was right. His necklace no longer hung around his neck. I guessed it made sense that Dr. James would take it away from him, as a way to keep him here, but there was still a sickening feeling in my gut.

"Okay," I responded, hoping I wasn't doing something that would destroy our team.

Seconds later we were back in the basement. Audrina, Samuel and Gave were now sitting up on the tables.

"Well, it's about time," Gave said.

"Sorry, did I take too long?" I responded. "I was trying to jump back to a minute after I left."

"Well, you didn't quite make that jump. You've been gone for an hour," Samuel said dryly. "We can discuss your little adventure in a bit. Right now, I want to focus on the fact that Theo is with you. How did you find him?"

"It's good to be back," Theo said, looking around the room and then raising his eyebrows. "Are we in the basement?"

"Yes," I responded. "We needed some place to hide and cover any energy."

"Good choice," Theo said, crossing to Samuel. "Dr. James has requested you pay her a visit."

"What does she want?" Samuel narrowed his eyes as he inspected Theo. I could tell he was silently questioning how Theo was standing here with all of us.

"She wouldn't tell me, but she had hoped it would be you trying to do the rescue and not Esa."

"That doesn't make sense," Samuel said.

"She told me she knew who was attacking the team and that you would find the information particularly interesting. She kept saying that if there was anyone who would appreciate the science, it would be you."

Samuel took a deep breath. "That's definitely true. I would like to find out more. However, we can't risk the entire team going and getting trapped there. Let me go alone. If I'm not back in a couple of minutes, you can come and find me."

"I'm not sure I like that idea," Audrina said. "Why don't I come with you?"

Samuel shook his head. "I don't want to take any additional risks."

Instantly, he disappeared on the Jump Line.

Chapter Twenty-Four

Chapter Twenty-Four

"Should we follow him?" Audrina snapped her head around to look at the rest of us. "It doesn't feel right to let him go alone. He may need one of us with him."

I grabbed Theo's shoulders. They felt different than before, as if he had been lifting hundreds of pounds. "Something's changed." I gulped. "What did she do to you?"

He jerked away. "Stop touching me!"

"Fine. Why does Dr. James want Samuel?"

He shrugged. "It has something to do with what you have been calling 'the Hunter' and her plans to trap it. That's all she told me."

"How is she going to trap something she can't see?"

"I don't get it. Why does she want Samuel when any of us could help her?" Nothing was making sense. Dr. James, Paul, Troy, Luther. Their names kept swirling around inside my head.

"What did she do to you while you were with her?" Gave walked up to inspect Theo. "Can you tell us what happened after you fell into the water?"

"I don't know. All I remember is falling backward into the icy cold. The water felt like thousands of tiny pins piercing my skin. When I awoke I was sitting in a room. Several people gave me blankets and food, but I didn't really see her. I only heard her."

"What does that mean?" I asked, but I already knew the answer.

"She would talk on the intercom and ask me if everything was okay. She mentioned she wanted to have me do some training, but then you arrived." He looked over at me.

"Hmm...that's not a lot of information," I said. "You've been gone for several days."

"Why do you say it like that?" Theo had an odd look on his face. I had never seen him make the expression before, but suddenly he looked like a lost little boy.

"It's nothing. I just wonder what she's up to right now. I feel like we should follow Samuel, but I don't want to put the team in jeopardy."

Just as I was staring at the wall behind Theo, trying to get some clarity, I saw it: a tiny little glimmer of light coming from Theo's cheek. It was the size of a pinhole, but it definitely caught my attention and made the hairs on the back of my neck stand on end.

Suddenly, I knew it had all been too easy. She had tricked me again, and I had brought the enemy into our home. This wasn't our Theo. This was someone, or something, else. I had to keep calm, but it was taking everything for me not to touch its face. I wanted to know why the tiny pinhole had been created, and what was underneath.

Audrina looked at me wide-eyed. I tried to tell her through my thoughts not to let on about what we were seeing. We had to get this version of Theo out of here. He had already seen too much, and we didn't know what he was capable of.

"Maybe we should go back near Artek, by the large water hole," I said nonchalantly, trying to see what kind of reaction my statement might get out of this thing standing next to me with Theo's face.

Fake-Theo looked me squarely in the eyes. "Are you trying to get me to fall into the water again? Why?"

"N-no," I stammered, caught off-guard by the tone of his voice. "Not at all. I just thought we might want to go up there and be on standby, in case Samuel needs us. We are all he has left."

"I don't want to go back there. I don't want to be anywhere near Artek. Dr. James is an evil witch." Theo spat out the words.

"What did she do to you?" I asked him, holding my ground, wanting to know what else this thing wasn't telling me.

"She changed me, Esa. She has been changing all of us!"

"What did she do to you?" I asked, a little louder this time. "Are you even the Theo Marcus we all know?"

"Yes! It's me. Do you really want to see what your wonderful Dr. James did to me?"

"Yes!" I screamed back at him, feeling as if I were about to lose my mind. "What happened to you while you were at Artek?"

Suddenly, Theo raised his hand. He slapped it hard against his chest, and then he was gone.

"Where did he go?" Audrina scanned the room.

"Theo? Are you still here?" I asked into the empty space in front of me.

"Yes," he responded. "Are you happy? This is what she did to me. She destroyed my life!"

"You're invisible." I rubbed my hand over the space in front of me. I couldn't see him, but I could definitely feel him. I traced his arm and then his shoulders, up to his head. I could feel him shivering.

"Esa, she's planning on doing this to all of us."

"No! She's definitely not touching me!" Audrina huffed as she swiped at a long lock of her hair.

"She's already started the transition on the two of you. It's only a matter of days before you become like me. She was able to speed up the process since I was being held in the lab, but I heard her talking...she's already put the serum in your bodies."

"That's impossible," Audrina said. "I wasn't being held there. I was held at OnyxFive, with Paul."

"No, you're wrong." Theo looked into her eyes. "You were both at Artek. That's why we couldn't find you. Paul moved your bodies back to Onyx-Five before you woke."

"How do you know that?" Audrina asked.

"Because I overheard a conversation between Dr. James and one of the other workers. They were talking about you. Don't you get it? Paul and Dr. James are definitely working with each other...against us."

Paul had told us that he could do whatever he wanted to us. We were no longer normal humans, we were special soldiers who had unfortunately been stupid enough to give up the rights to our own bodies.

"Esa, three years ago I overheard your parents talking about NorthStar. I tried to figure out what they were after."

"You went to NorthStar?"

"Yes."

"Why?"

"To find out what was going on."

"Did I follow you?" I asked, thinking back to Paul's earlier words about Theo visiting NorthStar.

"I didn't think you had until recently. Your mom tried to use me as the excuse for you being hidden in 2007."

Gave approached. "I guess I'm the unique one now. They haven't done anything to me."

We stared at each other silently.

"Hmm. I wonder if they are somehow increasing our abilities. It doesn't make sense to reduce them," I responded.

Gave shook his head. "If I know one thing, neither Paul nor Dr. James want to be behind Troy. They are all so competitive, they've destroyed one planet and now they want to go and destroy another."

"We can't let that happen," I said. "We've got to find a way to stop all of this."

"There's one way, Esa."

I could instantly see in Audrina's thoughts what she was trying to say. If we all disappeared, or died, then the scientists would have nothing, except for Luther. It was the one thing that we had over them...our lives.

"No, we can't do that yet." I looked back at Audrina. "There's too much at stake. There are other lives we need to protect. Besides, they seem to constantly be able to find us."

"That's right," Gave said. "We need to remove our trackers."

"I agree. I also want to know why they haven't created more soldiers. It seems like they would easily be able to do that," I responded.

"I've wondered the same thing about the team for a while. Why didn't they create more? But maybe they have. Maybe there are more soldiers; we just haven't met them yet."

"Who knows? I don't even want to pretend that I understand the way she thinks, or how she prioritizes things." My shoulders sagged.

Audrina let out a soft laugh. "Yeah, that's true. She definitely didn't have her priorities straight when she went and hid her daughter in a completely different year."

Theo said, "I really don't want to return to Artek, but I think we all have too many questions. Maybe we should go."

"The good news is, no one can see you," Gave said as he tried to figure out exactly where Theo was standing so he could slap him on the back. "I've missed you, buddy."

"Yeah, I can tell. I've missed you too," Theo responded. "Are we all ready? Esa, please do the honors." I tapped my medallion with two fingers opening the Jump Line. I nodded to the rest of the group, and then we all ran forward, unsure what would be waiting for us on the other side.

Chapter Twenty-Five

- -

Chapter Twenty-Five

Quadrant One's icy air greeted us. All around us was white snow and ice.

"Where is Artek?" I asked through chattering teeth as I wrapped my arms tighter around my chest, to protect my body from the cold that felt like a thousand little knifes on my skin.

Audrina studied the white landscape. "Sorry, we need to jump again. It's too far of a walk from here."

She tapped her medallion, we all jumped on the line, and suddenly we were in the cave where Audrina and Samuel had built Station One. The temperature was still frigid, but at least it was not going to kill us quickly.

We hastened toward the station's main door and Audrina typed in the code to unlock it.

After a loud click, the sound of pressurized air being released echoed throughout the cave.

Audrina looked over at Gave, and he took the lead and stepped through first. Then she turned to follow, but ended up hitting Theo.

"Ouch!" Theo grumbled. "Watch where you are walking."

"Sorry, I'm still getting use to the idea that you are completely invisible and we have no freakin' clue where you are," Audrina responded. "It's not my fault that I can't see you."

"It's not my fault either," he said dryly. "Just be a little more careful."

"Or you could try and not be so sensitive."

"Okay, both of you need to stop." I put my hand up in the air. "Don't forget, it might actually be a good thing that Theo is invisible. He might be able to get into Artek and do some surveillance work before we go."

"Sure. Sounds peachy to me. I recall saying, I didn't ever want to come back here, and now you want to send me back into the lion's den all by myself."

"Dude, Samuel is already inside," Gave snapped. "What happened? You turned invisible and became a chicken?" Gave was suddenly picked up and pushed against the wall. "Well, obviously this new you is also a little temperamental. Now, put me down." He was slowly released. "Theo, your personality has changed since we found you. I'll be honest, I don't really like this new you."

"Your personality would change, too, if everything you had worked for was suddenly different. Yes, I'm angry. I'm angry at all of you. You allowed this to happen!"

"No, we didn't," I moved my body in front of Gave, suddenly unsure if we had made the right decision to bring this version of Theo to Artek. He was different. Angry. He sounded like Luther had when I'd confronted him at NorthStar. At the time, Luther had also been fuming at Dr. James.

Suddenly, a table at the far end of the room toppled.

"Theo! Stop!"

"Stop what?" he responded smugly. "You guys don't want me to ruin your day?" His voice had gone from smug to sickly sweet in a sarcastic sort of way.

"It's not our fault this happened," I said, biting down on my lower lip. Even though I couldn't see him, I knew he was close. I could feel his warm breath on my skin as he leaned in.

"Be careful," he said softly.

"Okay."

Theo must have stood back. "I'll go see what's going on in Artek. I can already tell you that Samuel is probably being held prisoner, and we will likely all be captured and then used again for another one of her science experiments."

"Wow, this has not only made you angry but also pretty darn depressing," Audrina said, glaring at the empty space in front of her.

"I'm just trying to make you all aware of our fate. Don't blame me for giving you a dose of reality."

"Just go, and let us know what you find," Gave said. He then waited silently for almost a minute before clearing his throat and nodding. "Okay, Theo's energy is gone. I'm unsure what to expect next. Theo is different," he said. "What do you guys think?"

"I agree," Audrina responded. "He's a complete jerk. It took everything for me not to give him a swift kick in the butt."

"Me too," I agreed quietly. He certainly hadn't been the same Theo who had rescued me from the Hunter not too long ago. What if we all became this angry because of the serum Dr. James had put into our bodies? Theo also no longer had a medallion, but he was able to travel through time. I knew I should probably bring up that fact, but I decided to wait until I could talk more with Theo.

"Do you guys think we should wait for Theo to get back or just go?" Gave asked. "I personally don't know if we can trust any Intel from Theo right now."

"Let's go." Audrina glanced at me and then tapped her medallion.

We ran onto the line and ended up in one corner of the massive white room.

"Great. I'm pretty sure we just blew our cover." Audrina sneered. "Sorry, guys, I was trying to land someplace where we wouldn't immediately be seen, but I guess I'm not as good as I used to be."

We crouched in the corner.

"I'm not sure it matters. This entire place probably has motion detectors. If someone finds us, jump back to Station One and we'll regroup."

"Okay," Audrina and Gave both mumbled in unison.

Slowly, we inched our way toward the door. Just as I reached for the handle, the door swung open to reveal Dr. James.

"Very good. I'm glad the entire team is here. We need to talk. Follow me."

She turned and marched of the room. Meanwhile, we looked at each other, wondering what to do. Should we jump back to Station One or follow Dr. James?

I pointed my finger, indicating that we should follow her. We walked into what looked like a large conference room and Dr. James strode to the front.

"Please have a seat."

"Where's Samuel?" I asked, looking around to see if my brother was anywhere near, but he wasn't.

"He will be here shortly. I want to have all of you together." She turned to her computer just as Paul walked through a door at the front of the room. Samuel was escorted in by armed guards, who thrust him into the room and then departed.

"What about Theo?" Gave asked and then shook his head. "Never mind, I can tell he's already here."

"I'm glad we are finally all back together. It's been a long time—too long." Dr. James cleared her throat. "Let's get a few things out of the way. Esa and I decided she needed to go into hiding three years ago, so we could both have time to better understand what was going on and find our true enemies. With the help of General James, I was able to ascertain that Troy and Luther had been working together for some time. You can imagine how upset I was, to find that someone on our own team was a traitor.

"By disappearing and building Artek, I bought the planet a lot more time. Troy has not found Artek. Trust me, he's definitely been looking, but he hasn't been successful." A little smile pulled at the corners of her mouth. It was a look that made me cautious. How could I trust her?

"Now, we have a lot of work to do, so it's time for the games to end. I have been testing each of you to see how strong you really are for our next mission. I think you are already. Troy has been working on a project called Merak. I'm tempted just to let him go and get off this planet, but we have no choice but to stop him. He doesn't deserve to get to visit Merak."

"How do you know this?" I asked.

"Because, Captain James, I have been doing my homework. While you guys have been jumping through time, changing history, I have been busy working."

Samuel shook his head and laughed. "I think we all know we haven't been jumping through time simply for the sake of it. If you and General James had been honest from the start, we wouldn't have wasted so much time. We've been fighting off enemies for the past few years, trying to figure out what is real and what is not."

Dr. James stared at Samuel. "Fine. That's a somewhat fair statement, but now that I have you all here, it's time for us to clear the air and start looking to the future, not the past."

Theo's laughter filled the room. "That's easy for you to say. What have you done to us?"

"I was allowing you to take full form Theo. You should thank me."

"What!? Thank you? For destroying my life?"

"No, I have definitely not destroyed it. I have enhanced it. You can now travel anywhere without the medallion, and I mean anywhere."

"Then why didn't you test this on yourself or some other person instead of me?"

"Oh, it's been tested, don't worry about that."

"What happened to the normals you tested the serum on?"

"Unfortunately, they were casualties. This is war. People will live and people will die," she said, leaning over the table and glaring at all of us. "The one thing you all need to understand is that I am the most powerful one in this group. You will answer to me from now on. Do you understand? I am the leader and I command all of your respect."

Theo must have leaped across the table because suddenly Dr. James was thrown against the back wall. General James swung his fists several times, attempting to hit Theo, but he didn't have any luck.

"Run guys! Go!" Theo yelled at us. "This is a trap! I saw Luther and Troy in one of the other rooms!"

At the sound of those two names, my stomach dropped. They were here. Were they already working together?

"Go!" Theo yelled again as we watched him pound Dr. James and General James against the wall.

It would be only seconds before more guards arrived.

"C'mon," Samuel opened up the Jump Line. As we turned, Samuel reached back and pulled at something in the empty space. "You too."

Chapter Twenty-Six

- -

Chapter Twenty-Six

The team landed back in the basement. I knew, the minute we arrived, why Samuel had settled on this date and time. It wasn't a coincidence that the basement had been cleared out and provided cover for us. Knowing Samuel, he'd even put extra white suits down here for us to use.

Samuel looked around the room. "Where are you, Theo? I know you're here somewhere. I can feel your energy."

"I'm sitting in the chair. By the way, I don't like your mother. Just had to say that before you found me."

"Did you really see Troy and Luther at Artek?" Samuel asked as he approached the chair. It was odd knowing that he was there but being unable to see him.

"Yes. They were being held in a room down the hallway," he said. "I swear guys, I saw them. Luther was not invisible; it was definitely him. In fact, I'm pretty sure he was wearing the same outfit we saw him in outside of NorthStar the day we blew the facility to pieces."

"Why would they be there?" Audrina asked, tapping her fingers against her lips. "It doesn't make sense."

"It's probably one of the reasons we couldn't find Luther: Paul already had him. He set us up to destroy NorthStar, bringing Luther and Troy into the open where he could catch them. I guess we were being good soldiers. We had our orders and achieved our mission." Samuel glanced down at his clasped hands. "I know what you're all thinking: if this has happened, what else aren't they telling us. I'll be honest; I just don't know."

"Do we care that they have Luther and Troy?" Gave asked as he walked over to another chair across from Theo. "Let's think about it. It might be a good thing that all of them are in one place...away from us. It will also be easier to destroy them all."

"That's a good point," Samuel said. "I don't think we do. We just need to figure out what they've done to us and how we can destroy Project Merak. Obviously, it's not Troy's project any longer...it's Dr. James', and she has strong intentions of going back, I mean leaving this planet and going to Merak."

"What if Merak is the answer for our survival?" I looked around the room to blank faces. We needed to think about all sides of this story. Maybe it wasn't so bad. Maybe it was a way for us to live.

"You may be right Esa. Merak may actually be the answer that we've all been looking for. I've seen information about Merak. It looks like a strong choice. It has plenty of oxygen and vegetation for us to survive for many years," Samuel said. "However, I've tested this planet as well. We're fine. Civilization will once again populate. We just have to make some changes. I'm not really ready to just give up on Earth."

I spun back to face him. He was confusing. "What do you mean?"

"I mean, we need to make some changes. The current arrangement doesn't work out so well for all of us."

Finally, I cleared my throat. "Samuel, what do you really mean? Tell us honestly."

"We need to get rid them, Esa. Our parents are not like others. They don't care about us. They only care about their science. I think we've protected them for too long," he said as his head drooped. Soft sobs escaped his lips. I couldn't tell if they were real or fake, but either way he was my brother and very rarely had I seen him so vulnerable. It was weird seeing Samuel cry. "They've done this to us. They've manipulated us into doing their work and we really haven't gotten any credit for anything we've done."

The sound of the word "parents" caused me to take a deep breath. I wasn't sure I would classify them with that great a word. They were horrible human beings who only cared about themselves and how they could advance on their agenda. We were simply pawns in their weird game.

Suddenly, Theo's voice filled the space. "I agree with Samuel, we've got to get rid of both of them. Sometimes I wonder if you and Samuel are not also in on it." A thump, and a brief depression in the chair's arm, suggested he had punched the leather.

"Calm down, Theo. Don't worry, we get it. Didn't you just hear Samuel?!"

"Really? Do you get it?" he asked, as if he was unsure that Samuel had even spoken a few minutes ago.

"Yes."

"I don't believe you," he shot back. "I don't believe any of you. I'm starting to have serious doubts about this team. We were close at one time, but now I'm not sure we're all on the same side."

His words caused my heart to sink.

"Theo, what happened to you at Artek?" I asked, walking toward the chair where he was allegedly still sitting.

"Oh, not much. They just stuck me with needles and then decided to make it so no one could see me. It's been really fun. Super fun," he said. "I'm sure you are all jealous of me right now."

"I know I'm jealous," Gave said with an evil little smile, obviously trying to lighten up the mood in the room. "I keep thinking about all of the cool things I could do if I was invisible."

"Shut up," Samuel said. "Now is not the time for us to get distracted."

Gave's body rose off the ground. "Theo, put me down," he said matter-of-factly. "Seriously, dude, I was just joking around. You've got to lighten up just a little bit and stop pushing me up against walls. After all, Esa is finally back with the team. So, I really don't get why you are still angry?"

"Theo, put him down," I commanded. He didn't immediate respond. After what seemed like way too long he responded. "Fine."

Suddenly, Gave was back on the floor.

"Ouch!" Gave yelled, holding his arm. "I swear one day I'm going to make you pay for that."

"You deserved it." Theo huffed.

"That's not fair. You can't just go and hit someone, especially someone who has no way of fighting back. There are certain rules of engagement that we should follow," Gave said, stepping back from where he assumed Theo was still standing. "Wait a minute. We can't see you, but can you see the other invisible thing that has been hunting us?"

"No. I've looked, but couldn't find anything," Theo said. "I'm waiting for it to come back around to really see."

"But we now know it's not Luther." Audrina joined into the conversation.

"True," Samuel said, shaking his head. "Very true. Theo, did Dr. James send you on any missions before we found you? Maybe it was you traveling through time."

"That doesn't make sense. Why would I want to hurt you guys?" Theo's voice echoed. "Why would I want to hurt myself? Don't you recall, I fought off the thing too?"

"You were pretty mad at us just a little bit ago," Audrina said. "Besides, it doesn't matter. It could have been another version of you."

"Theo, it could have been you," I added, looking around the room.

I felt his body close to mine. "Esa, that thing hurt you. It really hurt you. I would never do something like that. I wouldn't do it."

"Maybe you didn't have a choice."

"I wouldn't have hit you."

"Esa's right, Theo. You may not have known what you were doing. Dr. James may have sent you out to find us and destroy us."

The entire room grew even quieter. It was eerie as we stood there and let the reality soak in that we were being targeted by several people, and, unfortunately, those people knew a lot about our hideouts and capabilities.

"The one thing I remember is Dr. James saying she wanted to make the team stronger. She said it over and over again, that we were weren't ready for the trip," Theo said.

Gave laughed. "Oh, I get it. She wanted to make us stronger, so she sent you to fight us, to see how strong we really are. Very nice. She's quite the peach."

"Theo, if it really was you, then you tried to drown me," Audrina said. "You tried to drag me to the bottom of the ocean."

"Aud, I swear, I don't remember any of this. You have to believe me," Theo pleaded. "I don't know what happened. All I remember is falling into the freezing cold water and then Esa coming to get me."

"There was a lot of time between those two moments," I said. "Anything is possible. Dr. James would have had time to send you on some of her personal missions. It's definitely possible."

"It is possible," Samuel said. "And I have a feeling we are right. It wasn't Luther. Dr. James wouldn't waste her science on him. She would want to use one of us, and I bet Theo was hand-picked for the job. You would never have accidentally fallen into that water. You're too strong and fast. Something pulled you in. Just like something led me to build a shelter in that location. I had no clue we were anywhere close to Dr. James or her facility. Everything seems so coincidental. Maybe she has been planning all of this and has guided us to make certain decisions."

"If that's true, then what's next?" I asked. "Do we wait and see if Dr. James sends us some sort of cryptic message?"

"It's time for us to get serious and figure out what Dr. James is really planning, and then we need to stop it," Samuel said.

Gave looked over at him. "Dude, if there's anyone who can stop it, it's you. I think we need to do some recon, but first we need to eat. I'm starving. Samuel, what are the odds we could sneak upstairs and get some food?"

Samuel laughed. "I think the odds are good since we have Theo."

"That's right! Theo, please go upstairs and pull out some leftovers. I'm sure I have something for us to eat hidden in the refrigerator."

"Fine," Theo huffed. "I'm glad to see my invisible body is good for something."

"Don't get caught," Gave said, looking over at the door. "I'd hate for something to lift your body up against a wall."

Samuel put up his hand to stop Gave from saying anything else. "He should be fine. I think the house is empty right now. I don't feel the presence of any other energy."

"Let's give ourselves a few hours to rest, but tonight we are going back to Artek," Samuel said. "It's time for Dr. James to realize she is not going to be running this show any longer. She gave us a unique skill set and its time that we used it."

Chapter Twenty-Seven

Chapter Twenty-Seven

The air was hot and humid. It felt like it was sticking to my body. A small bead of sweat made its way slowly down the side of my face as I pushed back a tree's low-lying limb. My heart was beating what felt like a million times a second. I looked around the tree-covered area. I had been here before. This place was familiar. Except, this time, I knew someone was watching me. I could feel their presence as their eyes lingered on my body, searching every part of me from my head to my toes. A sickening feeling came over me. Would I survive this time or die?

I wished I knew how to make time slow down. I could jump through time, but it was something that was always changing. At this moment, I wished there was a button I could press to completely stop time, so I could have a moment to really think about what was happening to me, to the team, to Theo.

The revelation that he might be the Hunter had left me feeling off. Memories of being thrown against the wall haunted me. I could still feel the pain in my arm as it struck the hard surface. Whatever had picked me up had wanted me dead. There was no doubt in my mind. It had come back repeatedly, and each time its main target had been me, except for in the hallway.

The Hunter had made his presence known, but he hadn't hurt me that time. He had killed one of Paul's guards. Had the Hunter changed? Maybe not. In the end, Paul and Dr. James had captured Audrina and me. Maybe that had been the Hunter's mission—to distract us and lead us right into enemy hands.

I shook my head, trying to clear my thoughts. I should be resting right now, not thinking of the past, but all I could do was pace the empty room. I needed to take control of this team and lead it, so that we were no longer on the defensive but on the offensive. This was our time to show what we were capable of. I knew the team was powerful. Individually, we had only shown some of our capabilities. Combined, we were effective and lethal.

Suddenly, I felt his large hands come down on my shoulders. Theo was standing in front of me.

"What do you want?" I asked, looking at the empty space in front of me and trying to visually see him, even though there was nothing to see.

"I'm not sure. I just wanted to be next to you. It's the only time I feel real," he said, guiding me to the couch. "Just sit near me for a little bit."

For so long I had wanted him to talk to me like this, but now didn't seem like the right time. "Really? You think that's wise right now?" I whirled around. I wanted him to look into my eyes and see the hurt and confusion. I had trusted Theo, and for some reason things had taken a drastic turn over the past few days.

"Esa," he pleaded. "I promise, it couldn't have been me who did all of those horrible things. There has to be another thing like me out there. I'm not the only one. Dr. James created more of these things. You have to believe me."

"I want to. Trust me, I hate the idea that you tried to kill me. It's not something that makes me feel good."

"Esa, you have to trust me."

"Trust. That's funny. Do you even know the meaning of the word?" He had told me on several occasions that he hadn't trusted me, but now he wanted my full trust? It seemed so ironic. Had he forgotten all of the things he had said and done to me over the past few weeks?

Theo didn't immediately respond.

"Theo, are you still here?"

"Yes."

"Why didn't you answer my question? It's frustrating that you get to pick and choose when you want to have a presence."

"Because I was thinking," he said softly. "Maybe you're right. Maybe you are all right. If so, there's something I need to do."

"What?"

"Goodbye, Esa."

"Wait! Don't go. We need you," I said, hoping he could hear the sadness in my voice. I didn't want him to leave again. I wanted him here...with me. "I need you, Theo."

Silence.

"Theo," I looked around the empty space hoping my eyes would see something that would bring me some calmness. "Theo, please answer me."

Silence.

"Theo, seriously, stop playing games," I pleaded, hoping he was just giving me the silence treatment, while he was thinking. Surely he hadn't really left me.

"Theo?"

Silence.

I walked backwards until I reached the couch, and sank into the soft leather as I looked up at the ceiling. It seemed like the entire room was spinning.

He was gone. I was alone in this room.

"Esa! Are you over here?" Audrina's voice cut through the quiet air as she suddenly came into view. "Oh, thank goodness. I was hoping you hadn't left."

"Why?" I said, closing my eyes. Theo's face filled my thoughts. I wanted to remember everything I could about him.

"Gave said he couldn't feel Theo's energy anymore. I wondered if the two of you had taken off somewhere."

"No."

Audrina studied me. "Are you okay? What's going on? Did Theo say something to you?"

"No. Everything is fine. Just like always."

"Seriously. What happened?" She demanded. "Where is he?"

"Theo was here. Then he said he had to leave. I tried to stop him, but he just left me. I'm not sure if I'm sad, surprised or mad."

"Hmmm. Did he say where he was going?" She asked, draping her arm around my shoulders to try and calm my shaking body.

I took in a deep breath and shook my head back and forth. "No, he just said he had something to do and then told me 'goodbye'."

"Something is definitely going on with him." Audrina pushed back a lock of white hair that had fallen into her eyes.

"Do you think he's coming back?"

She let out a soft laugh, "Of course he'll be back. Theo is a part of this team. He knows we need him. He can't leave us just yet. We're about to go on the attack. Besides, I've never known him to stay away from you. He loves you."

"Don't say that—"

"It's true. You're his entire world, but I don't think he understands his feelings. It's almost as if we are all wired weirdly. One minute we know how to love and the next we pull away. It's freaky, but Samuel does the same things to me that Theo does to you."

"Really? Speaking of my brother, have you talked to Samuel?"

"Yes. Samuel is working on some stuff. Like always. He is also the one who asked me to come over here and get you. It's time for us to meet."

"Okay. Can you give me about ten minutes? I need some time to myself to think and calm down. I just want to feel normal again, whatever that means."

"Okay." She rose. "Meet us down the hallway in a few minutes. Some quiet time may be good for you."

"I will."

As Audrina disappeared around the corner, I tapped my mcdallion. It was time for me to take a trip.

Chapter Twenty-Eight

Chapter Twenty-Eight

The field of vibrant flowers surrounded me. I had jumped back to the place I'd visited with Audrina, to get some clarity. The fresh air felt good in my lungs, and everything seemed so beautiful and peaceful. This was a safe place, I thought as I continued to drink in the scenery. My hands drifted over the tops of the flowers.

The idea of finding Theo seemed impossible. It would be like finding a needle in a really, really, really big hay stack. It was a crazy idea. This world was too big. Plus, I couldn't see his physical form or feel his energy. He had changed, and we didn't have a way to track him. I'd been stupid and naive to think I had any chance of finding him if he didn't want to be found. How would I even know if I were close? Was I just going to feel around the empty space, hoping to touch something that felt like his body?

He had the advantage over me. Theo could be anywhere. He could be standing next to me right now and I wouldn't know it. At least, I didn't think I would know. He was the perfect soldier.

The. Perfect. Soldier.

"Oh my god," I whispered, wondering if I had finally figured it out.

This couldn't be happening. If Dr. James wanted to create an army of perfect soldiers, she had definitely found the right recipe.

It was brilliant on her part, but also scary. If she changed all of us, our world would look very different. It suddenly dawned on me. Forget about traveling to another planet. She didn't want to go anywhere. She was planning on changing history. Everything was finally making sense. This had all been about buying her time to create the perfect soldier before she went back and truly changed the past.

I rubbed my aching temples. What if Dr. James had lied to us about Luther and Troy? Theo had said that Audrina and I had already received the serum, but I still felt the same.

I stuck my right hand in front of my face. I could still see it. When I swept my gaze down to my feet, they still looked the same. Thankfully, I had two legs and two arms.

My eyes suddenly darted back to my hand. It looked normal, but then I realized what had caught my attention: my pinkie finger was gone. I reached out with my other hand to see if I could still feel it.

"No!" I said to no one in particular. My finger was still there, I just couldn't see it.

The truth was sinking in, but I wasn't ready to tell the rest of the team. I needed to locate Theo and talk to him, but how in the world was I going to find someone I couldn't even see? What if I didn't have time and suddenly also became invisible? Would we ever find each other, or would I be alone?

I caressed my bottom lip as I continued to think about all that had happened. The past, present and, obviously, the future. If Dr. James was creating her "perfect" soldier then she was also tracking him. The idea brought a smile to my lips.

The only choice was to go to the one place where I knew I would find answers: Artek. Maybe, given the right incentive, Theo might make his presence known.

I touched my medallion, and was soon standing in the middle of a hallway inside the Artek facility. I hoped it was my primary year; otherwise, it would be a failed mission. I looked down at my watch. The year 2105 glowed on the small screen.

Artek's bare walls were now familiar. The sterile smell and emptiness greeted me like a swift punch in the gut. I knew the minute I arrived, my every move was being watched and analyzed by Dr. James.

"Hello mother," I whispered to myself. "I'm back."

My last statement made me quietly chuckle. I had seen a movie when I was stuck back in 2010 with that line.

There was no doubt Dr. James knew I was here at Artek, but I needed her to believe I wasn't entirely sure she had eyes on me. She needed to think I was still weak, but the truth was, over the past few weeks and months, I had come to know my previous self or at least what I knew of my former self. I was getting stronger and stronger every minute. My capabilities were constantly changing, but only for the better.

I crept down the hallway towards several white doors. They were close to the area where I had found Theo. Luther and Troy had to be behind one of them, but which? My pace quickened as I headed for the first door on my left. I had to find my targets before Dr. James approached me, and I knew that was only a matter of time.

Suddenly, there was a soft click at the far end of the hallway. My head whipped around towards the noise.

Dr. James strode swiftly into the narrow area and stopped at the other end. One of her hands was placed on her hip. The icy look she shot me caused me to shift uncomfortably.

We stood there staring at each other for several seconds. I clenched my fists. If she wanted a fight, I was ready.

There were no words to explain the overwhelming, sickening feeling that had crept from the pit of my stomach to the back of my throat. A part of me wanted to turn my head and throw up from all the emotions I was suddenly feeling as I stared at the woman who had given me life but who'd then kept trying to emotionally and physically destroy me.

My gaze darted around the empty hallway as my mind raced with plans.

"So, let me guess. You left the rest of your team to come here and find Troy and Luther?" Dr. James said, her voice echoing throughout the empty space. "I should have known the old Esa was coming back. You would do anything for the fight...even abandon your team."

"I didn't leave anyone. I'm not like you...Mother." I let the last word hang in the air. She needed to hear it. She was my mother. Flesh and blood.

I expected her to shoot back an immediate reply, but instead she turned on her heel and walked out of the hallway. That seemed to be her standard response when she didn't want to talk or answer questions. I looked at my hand. Three more fingers had turned invisible.

"Luther? Troy?" I whispered as I continued toward the doors.

Silence.

Suddenly, I felt a soft breeze.

"Theo? Is that you?" I whispered, glancing back down the empty hallway.

"Yes," he hissed, lowly. "What are you doing here? You need to leave...now."

"I came to find you and get some answers," I said, not slowing down. I had to find Luther and Troy.

"It's a trap, Esa. You've got to get out of here." I could feel his warm breath on my cheek.

"No. I'm not leaving until I find out the truth. Besides, if she is really looking to trap me, I don't know why she doesn't just do it," I responded, continuing toward the doors. I hoped that Dr. James couldn't tell I was talking to Theo.

"You have to go. Open the Jump Line and get out of here. Let me do this." I felt his hand wrap around my wrist. His grasp was tight.

Before he could do anything else, I yanked my arm hard and freed it from his grip. "I'm not leaving, Theo. Where are Luther and Troy?"

"The second door," he finally said, giving my arm a gentle squeeze. "Go home, Esa. Please. Let me take care of this."

"Where's home, Theo? Don't you get it? I need to be here. We've got to know the truth so we can have a home again."

"I know, but this doesn't feel right. If you won't leave then I will at least tell you to be safe."

The hallway suddenly felt empty again.

"Theo? Are you still here?" I whispered, but didn't get a response.

He was gone. He had left me alone. Again. I didn't have time to think about his actions. I headed to the second door. Checking down the hallway again, and then glancing toward the ceiling. She was up there somewhere, watching me. I knew it.

Without another second of hesitation, I pushed open the door, unsure what I would find on the other side. My hand instinctively flew up to my mouth.

"Oh my God!"

In front of me were at least fifty glass cylinders no more than seven feet high. Each was filled with some sort of water substance and a human body. These had to be the normals from NorthStar.

My legs felt weak as I moved closer to one of the cylinders...and then to the next one. At first I didn't recognize anyone inside of the containers, but then I saw her – my teacher from 2010. Her eyes were closed, but it was definitely Ms. Vaughn. She was in the first row, six cylinders back.

"I see you recognize one of them. All of these bodies will make perfect hosts." I suddenly heard Dr. James somewhere behind me. "Troy had promised me he was getting us strong specimens. I didn't really believe him at first, but all of these have been good so far."

"Are they dead?" I asked, unable to take my eyes off Ms. Vaughn. She looked peaceful as her body floated in the liquid. I kept expecting her eyes to open.

"No. They're not dead. At least, not yet."

"Why did you choose Ms. Vaughn?"

Dr. James laughed. "I watched her for a very long time and appreciated her attention to detail and the fact that she never grew tired of telling you to take off your sunglasses. I like strong individuals and she seemed like a perfect fit. I also didn't think she would be missed."

"You and Troy were always working together, weren't you?"

"Captain James, who I work with is none of your business. Trust me, it's very complicated and I'm not really sure you can handle hearing the full truth. At least, not yet."

"Wrong. I figured it out three years ago. Didn't I, Mom? That's why you sent me to 2007. It wasn't to protect your precious research; it was to protect your secret." It was all beginning to make sense. "You couldn't kill me, but you could ensure I wouldn't be found. That is, until you needed me again."

"I missed you, Captain James. You were never one to mince words. Like I've already said, you just don't get it. It's not that easy, but I am happy to report that all of my tests on you have shown that I've been successful and we can now leave this place."

"What place?"

"This planet," she looked as if she had grown bored of our conversation. That didn't really surprise me.

"So, you want us all to leave and abandon Earth when it needs us the most?"

"I don't really care about the future of this world. Besides, I have been helping out this godforsaken place for years. Who do you think came up with the idea to pull normals who were set to expire and provide their bodies to the people in the tunnels? It was me and it was a great idea that gave them many more years to survive. I'm not completely heartless."

I heard the soft thud of a pair of boots somewhere in the distance, and I scanned the darkness toward the back of the room. Paul quickly came into view.

"Hello, Esa." His white hair and teeth gleamed under the soft light.

I chuckled. "The first time I saw you, I knew there was something off. Your hair was jet black. It looked horrible, but that's because you dyed it so that we wouldn't know you had been on the Jump Line."

A smirk pulled at the corners of Paul's mouth. "Very good, Esa, but you still haven't figured out everything."

"And did you also know what mother did to me?" I asked him as I folded my arms across my chest. Had both my parents worked against me?

"Yes. It was necessary that you be taken away from the team so that we could test Marie's research," he said, rubbing his chin. "You have done very well and because of all of your work, we can finally go home."

"Home?"

"Yes, we have a home that we'd like to see again. This planet is boring and we've grown tired of being here. It has fulfilled its purpose. Now, we should go."

"What happened to Troy?"

"He will thank us one day. He thought too small, but thanks to us he will be able to grow much stronger and live a very long life."

Chapter Twenty-Nine

- -

C hapter Twenty-Nine

My bottom jaw dropped.

I felt the sickening taste of bile creep up my throat. The scene in front of me felt like something out of a weird science fiction movie, where humans are used in science experiments and then turned into aliens. I questioned everything I knew about my so-called parents and their passion for science.

"Well, I guess we now know Luther was not the Hunter, so that can only mean it was Theo all along. You sent Theo to kill me." I spat the words at both of them as my insides crumbled into a million pieces. Theo had tried to hurt and kill me...at the direction of these two villains.

"No, my child. You have it very wrong. I sent him to make you and the rest of the team stronger and more equipped to handle the future. To make you all fighters again. Look at your hand. It's working. We can adjust the mixture. When we get to Merak, you will see my full plans for this team and all of mankind. It will be beautiful. You will love Merak. Trust me."

I didn't want to listen to anything she had to say, but I couldn't help it—I glanced down. My body was still intact, except for my hand. It looked as if my arm stopped at my wrist, like I had no hand! "I don't want to be invisible. There has to be a way to reverse the serum. You can't do this to me. I'm your own flesh and blood." I pleaded with them; although, I knew it would be pointless. I doubted they cared about me or the rest of the team.

"Don't worry. You will adjust. That's your purpose." Her gaze snapped down to me. Her eyes had turned dark and cold. The hardened expression sent chills down my spine. "What we have done is cutting edge. It will be the biggest thing that has ever happened to the entire universe. We can't think small right now. We have to think about everything that is out there and trust me, what is out there is a life form so advanced it puts mere humans to shame."

"What? That doesn't make sense."

"Yes it does and you know it. I'm sure you are starting to see images of Merak in your head. It's your home too Esadore."

"Esadore? Who is that? My name is Esa. Actually, it's Captain Esa James. Not Esadore!"

I turned my head and tried to regain my composure. I wouldn't let her get to me this time. I had to be strong. Unlike what she just said, I was concerned with the past and present.

"All of the normal humans are dying off because YOU allowed Troy and General James to use them as test subjects. This war is your fault!"

"No! That is actually not true. The war was on the eve of erupting when we arrived."

"Arrived? What does that mean?"

"It means exactly what I just said. We arrived just before the war broke out. It worked out very conveniently for us."

"Liar! You all have a lot of blood on your hands."

She held up her hands in front of her face. "Funny. I don't see any blood. In fact, my hands look very clean."

Dr. James gave me a look that dared me to say something else to her. I could tell she wanted me to argue. To get mad. Anything to justify what she was doing at Artek, but then she began to laugh. The sound felt like I was listening to nails being dragged down a chalkboard.

"That's how your world works. Not mine."

Just as she started to lower her hands, a lone crimson droplet appeared on the outside of her right hand. It looked intense next to her ivory skin. Another quickly materialized right next to it, and both began to slide down her skin as Dr. James looked on in horror. Then a third appeared. And a fourth. Fifth. Sixth.

Dr. James suddenly let out a soft laugh. "Hello, Theo. I had a feeling Esa's presence would bring you here."

Silence.

"That's not Theo," I said defiantly. "That's the blood of all of your victims."

"Oh, Theo. You can stop playing games. We are already tracking you. I'm fully aware that you are standing right next to me."

"Good afternoon, Dr. James. My name is LUX," a familiar robotic voice said from somewhere in front of me.

I looked around, trying to see any sign of LUX, but the rest of the area remained empty. LUX? I asked myself. What would she be doing here? And then I knew.

"LUX!" I said a bit louder.

"Yes, Captain James, I have come to save you," she responded dryly.

"Thank you," I mumbled as I tried to think about my next move. Then it dawned on me. "LUX! Take out the power!"

"My pleasure."

An instant later, the room went dark. I inched toward the wall, hoping someone would make a move, and then I saw it: the same bright light I'd seen in the hallway. I watched in silence as both Dr. James and General James disappeared. They were going somewhere, together.

I reached instinctively for my medallion. I needed to get out of this place. If they were leaving then I needed to leave as well. I waited a few more seconds and then threw my medallion into the space ahead of me. Just as I was about to run toward the line, I felt the presence of someone near me.

"LUX? Is that you?"

"No. It's me. Theo."

The sound of his voice caused me to take in a deep breath. "Theo! You're here."

"I've been here the entire time, Esa. Let's go. We need to talk with Samuel."

"What about LUX?"

"What about her?"

"We need her too."

Suddenly, he erupted into laughter. "She's not here, Esa. It was me the entire time. Thank goodness for voice changers."

"Thank goodness," I mumbled in response, still thinking about the droplets of blood on Dr. James' hands.

Before I could blink, I was back in the basement. Samuel was pacing when I appeared. I knew Theo had to be with me, but we still couldn't see him.

"Oh, thank God, Esa! I was worried about you," he said, throwing his arms around me. "Where were you?"

"Artek."

"What? Why would you go there without the rest of the team?"

"Theo was with me."

"Then why wouldn't you tell me?" Samuel's eyes looked deep into mine. "I can't protect you if I don't know where you are at."

"The same reason why you wouldn't tell me the truth a few days ago about searching for Luther and Troy."

"What does that mean?" he asked, puffing out his chest.

"Samuel, I saw Troy. Dr. James has his body in a large cylinder."

"Still alive?" His eyes narrowed as he looked back at me.

"Yes, but I'm not sure for how long."

"Esa, come over here and sit down for a minute. Tell me everything you saw."

Chapter Thirty

Chapter Thirty

Flashes of lifeless faces invaded my thoughts. They would be hard to forget. It didn't matter what Paul or Dr. James had said to me; I knew they were already dead in all the ways that counted. There was no way they could recover and be normal again. A confused sense of fury and sadness coursed through my veins.

"I was in a room and there were large cylinders in perfect rows." I paused to catch my breath. I looked around the small space. Everyone was staring expectantly at me. "There had to be at least five rows of ten or so cylinders. Each contained a body. They were floating. It was horrible."

"And you saw Troy?" Samuel asked. His posture was rigid. "Are you sure it was him?"

Samuel and I had grown close over the past few months—there was no denying, we had a special connection—but despite our similarities, we were still different.

"Samuel, it was him. I know it. I'm complete certain I saw Troy in one of the cylinders."

"What else did you see?" Samuel asked.

"I don't know—some kind of fluid—but Dr. James said the people weren't dead."

"So, were they connected to some sort of breathing machine?"

"I don't know. I don't think so." I looked over at Audrina. She had moved closer as I'd told my tale. "Why are you so curious?"

"I just need to know exactly what Dr. James, I mean, our Mother, is working on right now."

"Fine. Yes, I think they were connected to something."

"Good. Maybe she has found a way to preserve the human bodies to be hosts."

"Wha—"

"I'm sorry. I shouldn't have said that," Samuel shook his head. "I was just thinking out loud. Ignore my previous comment."

"It's a little hard to do," Audrina said.

"I agree."

Samuel rubbed his hands together. "I'm sorry. I misspoke."

"Okay. Whatever. In the meantime, my hand—it's disappearing." I held up my arm to show them.

Shock flickered across Gave's face. The area below my elbow was completely gone. I could feel it, but as I continued to wave my arm back and forth, there was no way to see my wrist or fingers. The sight caused a single tear to escape and roll down my cheek. Soon I would be just like Theo: gone to the human eye.

Audrina held up one of her hands. It was hard not to stare at the gaping hole. "Esa, we're both disappearing."

I clutched the front of Samuel's suit. "You have to help us, Samuel. You can't let this happen to us."

He shook his head. "I think I may have come up with a something to reverse the effects of whatever Dr. James did to the three of you, but I don't know how well it works. I haven't tested it. I'm not ready to use it on any of you yet."

"Test it on me," Theo said from the other side of the room. "I have nothing to lose."

"What?" I couldn't help but yell back at him. "What about me? What about the team?"

"Esa, I can't have you this way. You can't even see me. No one can see me," his voice trailed off and then he gave a soft laugh. "Trust me, it definitely has its perks, but I didn't sign up for this. Besides, we now both know that it was me who came back and was physically hurting all of you. Why would you want me around anyways? What if I attack again?"

"Because you're family," Audrina said matter-of-factly. "Theo, you need to stop this pity party. You attacked us while you were under the influence of some sort of drug."

Theo huffed. "It's not a pity party, Aud."

"Call it whatever you want," Audrina said, looking around the room, trying to figure out exactly where Theo was standing. Suddenly, she was lifted off the ground.

"Theo! Put me down!" Her eyes widened as she stared down at her dangling feet.

The sound of Theo's laughter filled the room.

"I'm serious. Put me down...softly. Now!" Audrina playfully snapped. It was good to hear laughter, even if it was only a hint of it.

"Fine," he lowered her body. "Sometimes you all are no fun. I'm not planning on staying invisible, so this is my last real chance to have any fun."

"Theo Marcus, you are a jerk," Audrina the empty space in front of her body. "But, I'm glad you plan to show us your handsome face again sometime soon."

"Oh please, he's not that good looking," Gave walked over to Audrina with a smirk on his face.

"Gave! Take that back!" I playfully yelled in an attempt to try and show some respect towards Theo.

"Never!" Gave responded making us all laugh. It felt good to be with this group. Slowly, our laughter died down into silence as reality once again sunk in for all of us. Our laughter had been a brief distraction, but that was it.

"Samuel, let's do this," Theo clapped his hands. "There's no sense in dragging it out."

"We will need to go to my lab in Station One. I can't do it here. I don't have the right equipment," Samuel pointed around the room before tapping his medallion. Instantly, we were back at Station One.

Samuel began to rummage around with several different vials on his desk.

"I'm walking over to your table and will lie down on my back," Theo said from somewhere inside the room.

"Okay. I'll need to somehow mark your body so I know where to safely inject you," Samuel said.

"Where do you have to inject me?" Theo's voice suddenly had a hint of concern.

"The neck area would be best."

"Of course. Yes, let's put a needle in my neck. Let me guess...it's not a little needle, is it?"

"It depends on what you classify as little," Samuel turned towards a glass box and typed in a code. The lid slid back and my brother reached inside and pulled out an odd-looking rectangular device. As he grasped one end of it, the rest lit up in a series of different colors.

"What is that?" I asked, mesmerized.

"I don't have a name for it. Again, guys, I haven't really had much time to perfect this stuff. Dr. James developed it initially when she was doing some genetic research a few years ago. I saved most of the experiment and then modified it once I found out about Dr. James injecting you all with some sort of body-altering serum."

"Let's do this," Theo's said. "I don't want to think about this anymore."

Tears fell down my face, leaving wet streaks in their wake. I approached the table and felt for his hand. "We'll all be here while you do this."

"Thank you, Esa." His fingers tightened around mine. "You were awesome back there at Artek."

"Thank you," I responded trying to hold myself together. I needed to be strong for him.

Samuel walked over and placed small strips of tape on Theo's body. "Is this your ear?" Samuel asked.

"Does it feel like my ear?" Theo responded sarcastically.

"Yes. Don't patronize me. I have to ask these questions, just to confirm," Samuel continued to walk around the table. "I think we both want to make sure I hit my mark...the first time."

"Well, you're asking stupid questions."

"Fine. I'll be quiet and just hope I hit your neck area for the injection. Otherwise, I'll have to do two, maybe three injections. I guess practice always makes perfect."

"I want you to know that I think you're a big jerk."

"I don't really like you either," Samuel continued to place bright pieces of tape around Theo's body. "Okay. I think I have a pretty good idea where your head is on the table. Hold still. This will just take a second."

Samuel placed the rectangular object on the spot where he had marked Theo's neck. It made a series of short beeps and then one louder, much longer beep.

"Gah." Theo gasped.

Suddenly, the noise stopped. We all waited, unsure what was going to happen next, but everything stayed silent. I looked up at the clock and watched as different numbers flashed on its screen.

"LUX," Samuel said.

"Yes, sir?"

"Please scan his body."

"Will do." There was a pause for what felt like five minutes, but which I knew was probably much shorter. "His scans show no activity."

"Wait! What does that mean?" I looked over at Samuel.

Samuel studied one of the holographic images that had appeared, showing the outline of Theo's body. "It means there's no movement."

"Is he dead?"

"Yes. That's exactly what it means."

"You've got to do something!" I ran over to him and grabbed his arms. The second my hands touched him, I experienced an electric shock.

"Ouch!" I shook my hands, trying to forget the pain. "That really hurt this time."

Samuel gave me an odd look. "Did it hurt more than normal?"

"It felt like it did."

"Great. Now that we are changing, we are becoming weaker," Audrina said as she looked down at her boots. "I think Dr. James is intentionally making the girls on the team weaker so she has fewer of us to fight."

Samuel crossed to Audrina and reached for the hand that had already started the disappearing process. Her eyes widened when she realized what he was going to do.

"No!" She tried to pull her hand back, but it was too late. "Ouch!" Audrina wailed. "What was that for?"

"I wanted to see something." Samuel walked back to the image of Theo. "Hold on, Theo."

Samuel placed both hands on Theo's chest and sent several bolts of electricity through his body. The monitors changed for a brief second but then went back to showing a flat line.

"Samuel, do it again," I moved closer, uncertain if we were hurting or helping Theo. I hoped it was the latter.

Samuel looked over at me. "Esa, I'm not sure this is the right thing to do. We might be killing him instead of helping him."

"He's already dead. We've got no other options. Samuel, you have to save Theo. I don't want to live without him," I clenched my eyes shut and prayed for a miracle.

Samuel extended both of his hands over Theo and then plunged them down onto Theo's chest. "Sorry, buddy," he murmured as he let loose several strong bolts of electricity. The surge caused the outline of Theo's body to glow bright blue.

"Samuel, something is happening," I whispered, unable to take my eyes off the image in front of me. "Do it again!"

"Esa, it may be too much. I think we should wait a little bit longer—"

"Do it. Now!" I tried to muster enough courage to make them all believe that I was back in control. I willed my knees not to shake or give out from under me.

"I will do it one more time and that's it. His body can't take this much electricity."

"How do you know?"

"Because you told me my touch was more painful. Esa, I'm sending four times the voltage into him than I sent into your hand. It's a lot! It's enough to burn his insides."

"Fine. Just do it one more time." Samuel let both of his hands hover over Theo for several seconds and then he quickly thrust them back down onto Theo's chest. The intensity of the electricity caused Theo to glow even brighter, as if he had neon lights outlining the shape of his body.

We all watched for several seconds. The outline continued to glow brightly in the dark room, and then it began to fade. "No!" I shouted as I ran towards the table. "Samuel, you have to do something!"

Samuel came up behind me and wrapped his arms around my chest. "I'm sorry, Esa. There's nothing else I can do. I told you all, I hadn't tested the drug." Samuel began to shake. I knew he had finally let the best of his emotions get to him as he cried on my shoulder. "I'm so sorry. I'm so sorry," he sobbed. "I killed him."

I wanted to turn around and console my brother, but I couldn't. He was right. He had killed Theo.

Chapter Thirty-One

- -

Chapter Thirty-One

Tears stung my eyes as I stared at the floor, studying every line, hoping that something might jump out from the cool stone and eat me alive. Yes, a gruesome, horrifying attack would at least end the sickening feeling growing in my body.

I turned and shuffled toward the door, hunched as I tried to comprehend what had just happened.

"Esa!" Audrina wrapped an arm around my waist. "Theo volunteered for this. It wasn't anyone's fault."

"I know."

"We're all here for you. We'll get through this together."

"Wait! Esa! Look at the monitors," Samuel's gaze was locked on to one of the screens. "Something is happening to Theo."

I stared in disbelief. Surely I hadn't heard him say that Theo was alive. How could that be? All of the computers had shown that he had died. I glanced mindlessly at one of the monitors and saw a thin line bouncing across the screen.

Samuel was right. Theo was definitely not dead.

We all watched, wide-eyed, as the screen continued to show weird readings. Then we started to see something change on the table. Slowly, parts of Theo's body became visible again. It was his torso first. Then his legs. Finally it was his upper body and head.

His remained motionless, but we could see him again.

It felt as if all of the air had been sucked out of the room as we waited nervously. Samuel moved closer and touched Theo's hand. An electric shock passed between the two of them, and a smile crept across Theo's face.

"Don't worry, I'll definitely make sure to pay you back for that one."

Audrina let out a loud cheer. "Oh my gosh! It worked. It worked!" Tears began to streak down her face.

Gave also looked a little shaken. "You really gave us a scare...again. I'm hoping you can stay alive for a least a couple of years before giving us another. I'm not sure how much more I can take."

Theo slowly sat up and raised his hand. "Is this right, Samuel? Can I really see my hand?"

I couldn't hold back any longer. "Yes, we can all see you again. You're back to your old self."

He looked over at me sheepishly. Our eyes locked for several seconds. I knew we both had a lot to talk about, but that conversation would have to wait for a later date.

Samuel had a proud look on his face. "I need you to walk around the room for a bit and tell me if there's anything different about your body."

Theo obliged, but after almost an hour of various physical activities, Samuel was confident that the concoction he had given Theo had been effective.

"Esa, do you want to try it?"

I didn't hesitate. "Yes!"

I eagerly crossed to the table and lay down. Samuel walked through the same steps he had done with Theo. Again, it took the drug several minutes to work, but slowly my hand came back into view.

Audrina was the last one to get the serum.

We were finally all back together, and back to feeling somewhat normal.

"Now that you all are feeling better, we do have to discuss what to do about Dr. James and her sidekick, General James." Gave looked around the room. "This has to end, and it has to end now."

I couldn't have agreed with him more. If we didn't destroy them, they would destroy us all. It was too much of a risk to let them live.

Chapter Thirty-Two

Chapter Thirty-Two

C

I felt like a hardened soldier, ready to go into battle, as I stood off to the side, practicing creating a ball of electricity between my hands. I watched in wonder as it grew bigger and bigger. The electricity jumped and intensified with each move. It was beautiful. Powerful.

Gave and I had been practicing over the past few hours. It had paid off and I had once again become a perfect marksman. At least in practice. Now, I had to see how good I could be in a real situation. There was no doubt I was confident, but was I good enough to defeat my creators?

"I need to tell you guys something," I paused. "I saw Dr. James and Paul leave Artek. They disappeared somewhere. I'm really not sure what to expect when we arrive."

The two of them together seemed dangerous. Dr. James had the code for time travel and the serum to make someone invisible. There was no telling what other new experiments she had been working on over the years. Paul, meanwhile, had the codes to the largest research facility on the planet.

"Okay. We have no choice but to go and find out." Audrina looked down at her hands and created her own ball of electricity. Her eyes danced with mischief.

"Theo! Catch!" She threw the ball toward Theo. He put up his right hand like a baseball pitcher and caught the charged sphere. The electricity instantly disappeared into his body.

"Nice try, Aud. Better luck next time." He winked.

"Esa, can we make him disappear again?"

Theo rotated his shoulders and then shook out his arms as he waited for my response.

"It was a little boring around here without him."

"The quiet was good, not bad," Audrina quipped.

"All right guys. Let's get focused," Samuel said.

"What are we going to do with all of the bodies that are being held in those pods?" I asked, but what I really wanted to know was what we were going to do with Troy and Luther? Should we destroy them or save them?

"We don't have anywhere to put them, and we definitely don't have enough bags to transport them on the Jump Line. If we blow up Artek, there will be casualties," Samuel shook his head. He hadn't seen the bodies, so I knew he couldn't fully understand what he was saying. These were human beings...and they were apparently still alive.

"We kept them alive last time."

Samuel shrugged. "Yeah, and that didn't work out so well for us. They've all been gone enough time now that if there were changes in time, they would have already occurred. There's no sense in returning them and risk them remembering this place."

"Okay."

"Esa, are you sure you're ready?" Samuel cocked his head to the side.

"Yes. I've never felt stronger."

"Do you have a plan for if we need to make a quick exit?"

"If we get in trouble, let's meet in 2010 at the bridge," I said. That had been one place to which we had returned on several occasions. I knew I could easily find the landing spot.

"Too obvious. They will have that place monitored." Theo paced. "We have to go someplace new. Someplace they are unfamiliar with, so they can't find us."

He was right. 2010 had become too well-known, and obviously Dr. James and Paul had both been tracking me while I was lost in that century.

"I think it's pointless to plan anything." Audrina huffed. "Let's just see what happens when we get in there. There's a lot of stuff up in the air right now. Gave, do you have the remotes for the detonators?"

A thin smile came to Gave's lips, "Yep, sure do. I'm ready to rock 'n' roll."

I looked at both of them. "Gave, did you already place the bombs around the facility?"

He paused as an uncomfortable look crossed his face. "We put them there a couple of days ago. Actually, I had Theo do it when he was still invisible."

"That was a good move." It had been the right decision on the part of the team. "Anything else that you guys have done recently that might impact this mission?"

"No. That was it," Gave said.

"Fine. I'll take the lead."

My statement caused Theo's back to stiffen. "Esa, are you really ready to live up to that statement? You were our leader, but you haven't exactly been around for the past few years."

It only took me three seconds to wrap my hand around Theo's neck and push him against the wall. His eyes widened as the realization set in that I was physically very strong—stronger than he had ever thought.

I held him in that spot for several seconds before finally releasing him. "Stop questioning me and disobeying orders."

I didn't wait for Theo to respond. I was tired of talking. Instead, I pushed past him and marched down the hallway to try and find a quiet spot. I needed time to think right now. "Give me a couple of minutes," I yelled back at them.

Memories of the car accident flooded my thoughts. It had been more than three years since that day, but I could still hear the sound of the metal crushing metal. Several people had died in that accident. Maybe their time had been up. Maybe not. The rest of the team had gone back to fix the situation once they'd found me. I had never asked what had become of the people in the accident. Had they gone on to live long, prosperous lives, or had they died the next day? Whatever had happened, those people, at some point, had also lost three years of their lives—they just didn't know it. That was the thing about time travel; there was always the ability for a do-over.

"Hmm." I sighed as I sat alone, lost in thought. Time travel definitely had its pros and cons. It was too easy to make slight adjustments to get things to go your way. Maybe it was lucky that Dr. James hadn't been able to change more of us. If there were too many of us roaming around, we would be doomed. There was no doubt in my mind about that.

I looked at the floor beneath my boots. I was probably to blame for numerous deaths over the past few years. I just couldn't remember what life had been like before the accident. Many of those who had died were probably innocent and should still have been alive.

Images of Luther filled my head. I could identify with him. He had spent the past few years mad at Dr. James because of what she had done to him. His anger led him to become a traitor, and eventually it pretty much led to his death. He was now floating inside a large cylinder in of a research laboratory, hooked up to several hoses. A part of me wanted to think that he deserved his fate, but that seemed so harsh.

I should be even more upset about my situation, but instead I hated my parents so much that I felt separated from them. After all, I didn't really know them. I had no emotional connection to them. The only one on our team who might have any connection to them was Samuel.

Something was missing. I could feel a sense of uneasiness ignite inside my body, sending my nerves dancing. Like always, things seemed to point to Dr. James. Who was she? What was her end game?

And then I got it.

"Let's go." I motioned to the rest of the group as I pulled out my medallion, getting ready to open the Jump Line.

"Wait!" Theo said.

"For what?"

"We need to talk. I need to tell you something," he whispered.

I paused for a second, "Is this urgent? If not, we can talk when we complete our mission. Please don't confuse any of our previous feelings. We are on a mission."

A look of defeat crossed Theo's face for a brief moment and then he rolled his eyes and chuckled. "Fine. I agree. I'm kind of over it as well." The look on his face was almost a dare. He was challenging me.

"That was a completely jerk thing to say," I snapped back. "With everything going on, this is the time you want to talk?"

"Nope. Guess not. Let's go."

"Fine." I had one thought in my mind, and that was to get to Dr. James and put a bullet in her head.

Chapter Thirty-Three

Chapter Thirty-Three

We landed in the room with the large tubes. In the darkness, each of the glowing contraptions stood taller than six feet, illuminating perfect rows between them. I scanned the room and instantly found the familiar eyes of Audrina, who was standing slightly in front of me, but who had turned to look back at the group. She appeared shocked, and I knew I probably had a similar expression on my face.

The containers were empty. All of the bodies were gone.

I shook my head. A few minutes ago, I would have had a different thought sequence, but now things had changed. I hadn't seen this coming. I had assumed the bodies would still be here. How had Dr. James been able to move them? And, more importantly, why? We had put explosives around the building. Had she known and then lured us back here with the intention of killing us?

"Guys, I think this is trap. Let's get out of here."

"Hold on," Samuel said as he walked down one of the rows, looking at the empty containers.

What if Dr. James had finally found a way to alter all of the normals who had been in the tubes? She would then have more soldiers to add to her army. She would need more time in order to complete her experiments. That was the only way for this to happen.

Then the sound of deep laughter sliced through the silence. She was taunting us from somewhere. I peered into the darkness, but the room was empty. She had to be here somewhere, watching us, seeing the looks of disbelief on our faces. I craned my neck around the other side of one of the containers to see if I could get a better view, but there was nothing.

Suddenly, I was thrown backward. It felt like a large fist had crushed several of my ribs. My eyes watered from the surprise attack. I looked over at the rest of the team and noticed they were facing similar assaults, but I couldn't see anyone else in the room with us. We were under attack. There was no doubt about that. She had built an army of invisible soldiers and they had us surrounded. There was no way for us to escape. They would easily see the Jump Line open, and then we would have no way of knowing who had jumped on with us. Panic filled my thoughts. We were going to die.

I stumbled toward Samuel. My foot hit the hard ground just as I felt something block it from moving any farther. My head jerked around to the other side, but nothing was there. I paused for a second, trying to slow my panicked breaths, but it was no use. I tried to calm my rapidly beating heart. That's when I felt something, or rather someone, grab me by the waist.

A large arm squeezed tightly around my stomach. "Don't fight me," a deep voice whispered into my ear. "Just hold on."

Like hell I'll hold on, I thought as I gasped for air. The sound of a voice gave me just what I needed: a target.

As fast as I could, I lifted my right foot and tried to land a blow on my attacker's face or throat.

"Crap. Esa, stop. Just relax," the voice whispered angrily in my ear. "Try to look like you're fighting me, but, please, I'd like to keep my face intact."

I knew the voice, but I also knew that I couldn't trust Luther.

"I'm going to kill you." I seethed as I plowed back my elbow as hard as I could. "Somehow, I'm not surprised to hear that you are, once again, turning your back on your team."

Luther's grip only tightened. His strength had definitely increased. His body was rock hard. Before I could blink, he had the rest of the group in his grasp.

"Now, Theo!" he called.

My gaze snapped toward Theo. Had he gone against us too?

There was a bright light, and Theo quickly put a hand on me, reaching the other toward Audrina and Gave. A strong bolt of electricity passed through me. The pressure caused my knees to buckle and then suddenly everything was dark.

***

I woke staring into a bright light.

"Am I dead?" I asked no one in particular. I really didn't expect an answer, but suddenly Theo's head appeared over mine.

"Esa, we need to talk about what happened."

"What? Where are we?" I asked groggily.

"Don't worry about that right now. I need to explain something to you."

I stared back at him in disbelief. Even through my anger, I found it difficult to tear my gaze from his eyes. I watched him for several seconds before squeezing my eyes shut again. This had to be a bad dream.

Theo shook my shoulders. "Esa, wake up."

"What?" I mumbled with my eyes still closed. There were so many questions swirling around aimlessly inside my head.

"How do you feel?"

"Tired. Mad. How about you?" I slowly sat up and rubbed my shoulder. There was still a dull pain in the area where Theo had sent a bolt of electricity ripping through me.

"I figured you might be a little upset."

"I'm not just a little upset, I'm really angry right now." I knew Theo had been behind that attack at Artek. He couldn't deny it. I had heard Luther and then seen Theo.

"I'm sorry."

"Where are the others?"

"In another room. I wanted to talk with you first."

"What about Samuel?"

"We haven't seen him."

"Where are we?"

"In the year 1965."

"Really? Why?"

1965 was the year in which I had thought Luther was hiding at one point. There had been a lot of energy emitted from that year.

"We finally put all of the pieces together." He looked down at his hands. "I'm sorry, Esa, but I saw more than I told you when I was invisible. Dr. James sent me on several missions, including the ones where I attacked the team, but then she also sent me to find Luther and Troy. I easily found them, and I also learned the truth."

"Well, it's about time. Theo, why couldn't you just tell me?"

"I tried to talk to you, but you pushed me away. Remember?" He arched his eyebrows.

I remembered it now. He had wanted to talk before our mission. "So now you're on the same side as Luther?"

"We're all on Luther's side. Don't forget, he's a part of this team. Besides, I knew he hadn't intentionally gone against us. It just didn't make sense. One minute he would be goofy and normal and then next he was completely different. Then, when we started questioning if I was the one who'd attacked the team, I figured it out. Just like me, he had been given something to alter his state of mind."

"Okay. We knew something was up with him," I looked into his eyes. There was something more that he wasn't telling me. "What else? I can see it in your face. You're keeping something from me."

"I don't think we're human."

"That's not possible. We look and act human--"

"We've been nothing but guinea pigs for these jerks. Esa, think about it. Where are my parents? Where are Audrina's parents? And, none of us have aged in years. We all look the same since we were changed."

My hand flew to my mouth. "Oh my God. I hadn't really thought about that."

"We all died in the Century War. The radiation from the Jump Line didn't cause us to change...Dr. Marie and General Paul James did this to us. We were the first normals they tested. Apparently, we are officially called "Ciphers." I'm not sure what that means, but Dr. Marie hasn't changed more of the normals here into Ciphers because she's saving their bodies for Merak."

I thought back to Luther when we had seen him walking outside of North-Star. His eyes had looked dead at that time.

"I've taken out all of our trackers. Dr. James can no longer follow us."

I looked down at my wrist. My watch was gone.

Theo nodded. "Our watches are gone too. We can't risk it anymore. This is a new day and we have to take more precautions. For the past five years, Dr. Marie and Paul James have led us through a series of obstacles and lies to test us. Not because they were trying to make us stronger, but because they wanted to tweak their research. It's always been about starting over in their new world."

"Where is Dr. James right now?"

"I don't know, but I'm sure we will hear from her again. For now, I have decided it was time for us to get away to a safe place. We anticipate the three of them will try to get to Merak very soon."

"She's still alive? I thought we were going to blow the place?"

"We did, but she was able to get out in time. We saw the bright light just as we were leaving too."

My eyes shot open. "I saw that light."

"I'm not sure where she is at right now. We don't believe there's another transportation mechanism to get to Merak. There's no way to simply jump to the new planet. It would mean jumping into the future, and that's not possible."

"Where's Luther?"

"He's here."

"Where?" I peered around the dimly lit room.

"Hello, Esa," Luther said from a shadow in the corner. I saw his bright blue eyes staring at me in the darkness.

"Hello, Luther."

"I'm sorry if I hurt you."

I rubbed my hands together. "I'm fine. Are you guys sure Samuel is not here?"

"Yes. Why?"

"I think we need to find him. He is just as smart as Marie. I know he has been hiding the truth from us. There is no way he could have known we're not human. I don't think he's just a bystander any longer. He's one of the enemies."

|$(H}

The Next Chapter

Thank you for reading Time Hunter! The third book in the series, Timed Out, can be found at: https://www.wattpad.com/story/11 8707897-timed-out-book-3-jump-line-series.

Of course, I would love for you to leave some feedback before you continue on to the next book. It's always great to hear from readers! Thank you! - Darcy

Timed Out

Https://www.wattpad.com/story/118707897-timed-out-book-3-jump-line-series

Chapter One

I slowly sucked in a deep breath and then thrust my head back underneath the steady stream of water. The heat and energy felt good, almost as if it were charging my tired body. It was just what I needed right now to get lost in my thoughts.

So much had happened that it was hard to comprehend. I was dead. Literally, I was killed five years ago and then made into Cipher. We looked human and could think on our own and feel emotions, but we weren't fully human. At least, that's what the woman who at one point I called "Mother" finally admitted. I was nothing more than someone's sick science experiment. I still didn't even fully understand exactly what I was made up of or how much of me was human.

Theo had told me I only had five minutes to shower and change, but I didn't want to get out. Besides it wasn't like we had anywhere we really needed to be right now or that we could truly hide from her. She always seemed to know our every move. We had removed trackers that had been embedded in our bodies, but still she found us.

This shower was the one place I felt somewhat real. I could feel the water roll down my skin. That had to mean something. How could I be dead? My mind had been on overdrive since we had arrived here, racing from everything that had happened over the past few hours. The one consistent link to all of the bad things in my life right now ...Dr. Marie James.

No one was safe. Not even me. At one point, we had apparently been her greatest invention, but then we began to think on our own and we disobeyed HER orders. Dr. James' skills had gotten better, but not good enough to completely dismiss us. She still needed the team. That was obvious, but why?

I felt my torso begin to convulse again as I dry heaved towards the marble wall in front of me. I hated her.

"I am going to destroy you Dr. Marie James," I whispered to myself as I tried to suppress the reflux to gag again. I knew she couldn't hear my words, but I didn't care. She had done too much to sabotage me over the past few years. At first, I had been led to believe that my biological mother had done these things out of love and a need to protect, but I was quickly realizing that idea was all wrong. I mean, it was crazy how off I was about her. She didn't care about me. For her, it was about control... and revenge. I was just a pawn in her little game.

I turned around and let the soft pellets of water slide down my back. I would have liked to be able to enjoy how the water felt, but I couldn't. Steam rose around me, so it had to be hotter than I normally liked it, but my body felt nothing right now.

LUX's voice interrupted the silence. "Captain James, the rest of the team is waiting for you to finish. How shall I respond to them?"

"Tell them I'm busy and don't have any plans to finish just yet." I thrust out my arm and let the water spray towards the glass door.

LUX didn't seem to fully hear my response. "Shall I tell them you will be going to your preparation tube within the next few seconds?"

"No." I quickly responded. I still needed more time to process everything. "Didn't you just hear me? I'm not getting out."

"Captain James, Theo has asked for an answer."

"I gave you my answer," I grumbled, letting my head fall forward. Theo could wait a few more minutes. I deserved and needed this time to figure out what was going on.

LUX's face disappeared from the screen. I closed my eyes again and let the water slide slowly down my cheeks...and then it was abruptly shut off.

"LUX! Turn the water back on!"

Silence.

"LUX!! I order you to turn the water back on! Right now! I'm the commanding officer and this is not funny!"

Before I could yell anything else, Theo appeared inside of the shower. He was standing only centimeters away from me, wearing his white suit with a serious expression on his face. In a normal time, I probably would have tried to hide my naked body with my hands, but I didn't care right now. We weren't real anyways. We were artificially created.

"What do you want?" I glared back at him. Theo needed to explain why he thought he should be standing in front of me.

His eyes looked back into mine. I felt as if they briefly softened before narrowing.

"It's time to go. I told you we only have thirty minutes," his fists clenched next to his body. "It would be nice if just once you would listen to me. I understand you outrank me, but I know this team and I know what's best for us right now."

"I heard you, but I don't care. Besides, it doesn't matter. Don't you get it, we're all dead. We really have no purpose other than to give her some sort of joy that she created us."

"Esa, you need to get dressed." His face was stoic as he stared straight ahead not even acknowledging my last few sentences.

"You shouldn't have jumped into my shower," I seethed, hoping he could hear how angry I was at the fact that Theo had violated my privacy.

"Go get dressed," he demanded, his serious voice rising several octaves. "Now! I'm not in the mood to play games."

"No," I responded defiantly. I really didn't care what else he had to say. He couldn't do anything to me. I was the captain of this team. He should be obeying my orders. "I'm not ready. I need more time. This shower is the one thing keeping me sane right now. It's almost as if the water is making me stronger."

"Esa."

I grabbed ahold of his face. He needed to see just how strongly I felt right now. "Theo, look at me. Trust me, this is not a game. Give me a minute."

"Oh, I get that. Do you?"

"Yes. Now, go away." I let my hands fall from his face.

His head slowly turned away from mine. For a brief second, it looked like he realized just how crazy all of this was for us.

"No."

"Fine. Then please just give me a few more minutes. I'm trying to figure out what is going on," I pleaded. It was all too much for me to try and figure out in such a short time.

It took him several seconds to respond. "Alright, but I'm going to stay in here with you," he leaned up against the opposite wall and looked upwards.

His words caused me to laugh from the absurdity.

"Okay, but close your eyes. It's a little weird that you are wanting to stay with me in the shower."

"No. I want to make sure you don't try and leave us once again. I'm in no mood to go searching throughout a whole bunch of decades to find you Esa. The team needs you right now. I need you."

"Fine," I turned back around. "Can you tell LUX to turn the water back on? She is obviously not responding to any of my commands, which is something we will address at a later time."

Theo shrugged his shoulders. "LUX, turn the water back on. Captain James will have one minute and then she will be done."

The water instantly came back on. Theo was quiet as I continued to let the water flow down my body.

Slowly, I peeked back over my shoulders. I guess I shouldn't have been too surprised. Theo was leaning against the far wall with his arms crossed over his chest, staring outside of the shower.

"What are you thinking about?" I asked annoyed he was giving me the cold shoulder...again.

Theo's presence in the shower was annoying, but also a distraction.

"Esa, don't," he said.

"Don't? What does that mean?"

"It means I'm in no mood for your constant questions."

His words hit me hard. They seemed so cold and mean. Once again, Theo was pulling away from me. Somehow I shouldn't be too surprised, but I was.

"Don't be an idiot," I turned back around and walked towards him. I slowly put my hands up on his face. "We need each other."

His eyes held mine and finally he responded, "I agree, but that might not be enough."

Suddenly, he walked towards me and put his finger on my lip. "Stop talking. We're not alone."